HIS DREAM ROLE

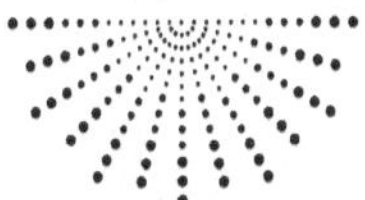

SHANNYN SCHROEDER

*J*ust as Free Mitchell parked his car at the health club, his phone started buzzing with a text. He should've called Cary as soon as he'd known he'd be late.

Are you coming?

Parking now.

Free ran around to the front of the building, where he knew he'd find his brother waiting outside. Even after all these months, Cary still wouldn't go in without him.

"Sorry I'm late. You could've started without me. It's not like you need me there anymore."

"I know. I like the company. So what made you late?"

"I was with Hunter and Adam talking about the New Year's Eve party."

"Let me guess—you had to wait on Hunter."

"Of course." Free reached over and pulled the door open.

As he walked through, Cary asked, "How'd it go?"

"The usual. Hunter wants a big blowout like

last year, but Adam and I don't. Hunter said he'd limit his invites if Adam and I have dates."

Cary laughed. Like out-loud-drawing-attention laughter.

"It's not that funny," Free said as they entered the locker room.

"You haven't had a girlfriend since last spring."

Free couldn't argue because his brother would know if he lied. He hadn't even had a real date since Kim broke up with him. He blamed being out of practice; he and Kim had dated for over a year. In reality, he sucked at asking girls out.

Cary changed quickly while Free waited. He never did a real workout with Cary. He was there just for the wow factor. As Cary grabbed a towel, Free adjusted the lapels on his coat and straightened his earflap hat. Showtime.

Some costumes he wore required more props. Sherlock Holmes was simple. Unfortunately, many people didn't necessarily get it, even with the overcoat and hat, so he carried an oversized magnifying glass with him to aid in his sleuthing.

Truth be told, Cary no longer needed his help. Last summer, after the doctor told Cary he absolutely had to get off his fat ass and lose weight, Free offered to work out with him. Cary admitted that it wasn't the working out that bothered him as much as the people staring at him.

So three days a week for the past six months or so, Free dressed in outlandish costumes to draw attention away from his overweight brother.

Cary sat down at the first machine to work his legs and Free leaned against the adjacent machine.

For a change, the room wasn't crowded and no one took notice of them.

"What are you going to do about Hunter?"

Cary talking to him during the workout was a relatively new development. For months, they walked in together, but Free would stroll through the gym drawing attention to himself in subtle ways. Over the last month or so, they'd spent more time hanging out during Cary's workout. Soon, Cary wouldn't need him to show up at all.

"I'm going to prove him wrong. I'll find a date for the party."

Cary extended his legs and brought them back. "See if she has a sister, okay?"

The workout routine continued on in the same manner, Cary working various muscle groups and chatting. They talked about work and the holidays and Free soon became bored.

When Cary got on the treadmill, Free wandered around, trying to find something of interest. Two muscle-bound guys came out of the locker room and sneered at him.

One said, "Who do you think you are?"

Channeling the arrogance of his father, as he did every time he needed to portray Holmes, he answered, "*I'm a high-functioning sociopath. Sherlock Holmes.*"

He cocked an eyebrow and waited for them to respond. The first guy elbowed the other and they called a few friends over.

A ball of nerves plummeted through Free. He'd never been much of a fighter and he knew he couldn't hold his own with the first two, much less all their friends. He looked at the group and said in his best British accent, *"I dislike being outnum-bered. It makes for too much stupid in the room."*

To his surprise, all the guys started to laugh. Sure, he was insulting them, and he was pretty sure they understood that, but they still laughed. Free pulled out his magnifying glass, nodded to them, and walked back toward the treadmills.

Cary slowed his pace. "Problem?" he asked, tilting his chin toward where Free had come from.

"Nope. Just my winning personality creating more fans." He leaned against the rail of the tread-mill while Cary jogged and watched the TV in front of them. Cary had it tuned to the financial reports. Free didn't need to hear the anchor or have closed-captioning on. He simply watched the numbers scrolling at the bottom of the screen. The red and green digits soothed him like a lullaby would a baby.

When Cary stepped off the treadmill, Free fol-lowed him to the locker room. "I'm going so I'm not late for rehearsal, okay?"

"Sure. See you later."

He walked out the front door of the health club, but instead of heading to the parking garage around back, he went to the coffee shop down the street. For the last month, there was a woman who came in at the same time he did. Samantha—he loved places that made it easy to learn everyone's name. In light of Hunter's challenge to get a date, and Cary's laughter at the thought, Free decided that today would be the day he would speak to her.

He entered the shop and a warm blast of air hit him. The shop wasn't usually busy at this time and today was no different. As he approached the counter, Samantha was in front of him, digging through her purse. The cashier watched her with impatience just short of rolling her eyes.

"I'm so sorry. I know I had cash in here." Her long, light brown hair created a curtain across her cheek. "I can't believe they stole it again."

For a change, things actually worked in Free's favor. He wouldn't need to force an introduction. He pulled out money and said, "Here. Let me."

The cashier smiled brightly at him. "Anything for you?"

"Large black. Thank you."

She charged him for both coffees and Samantha stared at him with her wide, pink-lipped mouth hanging open. He had the sudden urge to feel those lips against his.

"Thank you," she finally managed. "I can pay you back."

"No big deal."

From the other side of the counter, the barista called, "Samantha."

Free pointed over his shoulder. "Your coffee's ready."

She took a step, then paused. "How did you know?"

He winked at her. "Elementary, my dear. I'm here at this time three days a week. They call your name every time."

"Hey, Sherlock." The barista thought he was funny.

Free followed Samantha to the other end of the counter and grabbed his cup.

Samantha smiled. Her whole face brightened

as she looked up at him, her amber eyes shining, and said, "Thanks again. I appreciate it. I'll get yours next time I see you."

"Until then." He gave her a tip of his hat and turned to leave. If he had his way, he'd be sharing a cup of coffee with her by week's end.

As the bizarre Sherlock Holmes pushed the door open and held it for an elderly couple, Sam surreptitiously snapped a photo on her phone. She sat at a table and texted her best friend, Jess. **Guess who just bought me a cup of coffee? Sherlock.**

A minute later, her phone rang. "Hey, Jess."

"Where do you find the weirdos?"

"I'm at the same place I always get my coffee."

"And Sherlock Holmes just walked in and bought you a cup of coffee."

"My ten bucks was stolen out of my purse again." As soon as the words left her mouth, she wanted to yank them back because Jess was going to start yelling.

"Jeez, Sam, we talked about this. When you're at the shelter, you need to lock up your shit. I get that you want to help people, but that doesn't mean they won't steal from you."

Sam sighed. She did know better. She'd mostly learned her lesson her first week when her whole purse went missing. Now she only carried a small amount of cash on her, and bottom line, she figured if a kid stole it, he needed it more than she did. "I know," she finally huffed back. "Anyway,

Sherlock came up behind me and paid for my coffee."

She took a sip and waited for Jess's reaction.

"So, does he think he's really Sherlock?"

"Hmm…I don't think so. I've seen him in here before. He's always dressed strange, like in costume. Once he was Riddler and another time, a Jedi? And then again the guy with the pointy ears from the other show."

"So he's a supreme weirdo."

Sam smiled. "He was nice. He bought my coffee and left. He's cute."

"Oh God. Please tell me you didn't give him your phone number or make plans for a date."

"Nope." She knew better than to tell Jess that she planned to buy him a coffee as a thank-you. Jess might be right. He could be a total weirdo. In fact, the first few times she saw him, she was concerned that he might have some mental issues. But his costumes were too well crafted and he functioned well in public, so she figured he was just eccentric.

"I mean it, Sam. Find a normal guy."

Sam choked on her coffee. After clearing her throat and regaining the ability to breathe, she said, "I date normal guys."

"You intentionally find strange ones just to piss off your dad. You're getting a little old for that."

"Whatever. I gotta go. Talk to you soon." She disconnected quickly because Jess had known her long enough to know that was exactly what she'd done for years. Her dad had an idea of the kind of guy he wanted Sam to be with, so Sam rebelled. However, Sam really did like the guys she picked.

At first. She tended to fall hard and fast. It was her nature.

Sherlock was different. He was far from a bad boy. Maybe sweet and quirky was her type. Everyone had a type, right?

She finished her coffee, tossed the cup, and bundled up for the cold. As she exited the shop, she looked toward her car and wished she could abandon it. The Mercedes made her stick out everywhere she went. She believed the damn thing was the reason kids at the shelter were okay with stealing from her. The car screamed *I'm rich!*—which she wasn't. Her parents were well off, not her.

The car had been her compromise. She'd wanted to live in the city to be closer to the locations where she would work and where she currently volunteered. Her parents flipped. They couldn't have their baby living in unsafe situations and—gasp—taking public transportation.

They ultimately came to a compromise on an apartment, and Sam agreed she'd use the car to get to and from classes and her volunteer work. When she'd agreed, however, she'd imagined a regular car, like a Civic or RAV4. Her dad's compromise was getting a low-end Mercedes, as if one actually existed.

She pressed the key fob to disarm the car and got in. Admittedly, she did enjoy the heated seats when the weather turned. That probably made her a hypocrite.

The problem was, she wasn't quite sure who she was supposed to be yet and graduation was looming. Part of her wanted to continue on for her master's degree immediately so she could stay in her safe cocoon of school, where she knew exactly who she was. A bigger part of her, though, loved the work she did at the shelter, and she felt like she belonged there, like she made a difference.

She had a hard time reconciling the Mercedes-driving, heated-leather-seats Sam with the woman who wore yoga pants splattered with finger paint.

Sam pulled into her parking spot in the lot behind her apartment and sat in her car for a minute. A nagging feeling had been gnawing at her for months. Her life felt unsettled in a way it never had before. Jess's point about her dating habits hit home. She needed to decide what she really wanted and why.

The problem with that was she was going to a school, driving a car, and living in an apartment her father paid for. If she took the stand that she wanted independence, was she willing to walk away from everything that made her life comfortable?

Two days later, as Free was leaving the health club straightening his tie, Cary called out, "Hey. Before you go, I gotta know. What's going on that you pulled out Doctor Who? You usually save him for special occasions."

Free slid into his brown overcoat. "I have to see a girl about a cup of coffee."

"Seriously? Does she have a sister?"

"I haven't asked. And even if she did, I'm not working on getting you a date."

"Come on. Hook me up."

Free waved at his brother. "Later."

Minutes later, when he walked through the door of the coffee shop, Samantha was standing near the entrance. Waiting. For him? He smiled. "Hello again."

She eyed him up and down, taking in his pin-striped suit and his red Converses. He extended a hand. "I'm the Doctor."

"Doctor who?"

"Exactly." He turned toward the register. When the cashier looked at him, he ordered his usual black, no cream, no sugar and a large caramel macchiato for Samantha. As he reached for his wallet, she jumped in front of him.

"I've got this. I owe you for the other day." She paid for the drinks. As she tucked her wallet back into her purse, she turned to face him. "So really, what costume is this?"

She didn't get it. "*Doctor Who*. British TV show. Time Lord. Daleks. TARDIS." He watched her face for any sign of recognition. He found none. Sweeping a hand over himself, he added, "I'm the tenth doctor." Still nothing.

"I think I've heard of it." She smiled. It was enough to make his day, even if she was clueless about *Doctor Who*.

When their coffee was ready, he handed her the cup and was at a loss for what was supposed to happen next. He sucked at this.

Samantha pointed toward a table. "I have my books over here if you want to sit."

"*Books! The best weapons in the world!*" As soon as he said it, he knew it was a mistake, but once in character, he couldn't always stop. And the Doctor's words always sounded better than his own.

Samantha giggled a little. "I agree with the sentiment, maybe even your enthusiasm. It's one of the things I try to get across to the kids I work with."

"Kids? Are you a teacher?" He followed her to the table, knowing he couldn't stay long because he had to go to rehearsal, but he wanted to hear more.

"No. I'm studying to be a social worker, so I volunteer at a shelter for victims of domestic abuse. I see a lot of kids who are utterly hopeless, so I try to give them some hope, teach them that things can be different." She sat and slid her books toward the edge.

He took the seat across from her and waited. He hoped she would continue the conversation. She sipped from her cup and then licked a bit of foam from her top lip. Free stared at the tip of her tongue and her pink lip, entranced. Then she smiled again.

"You're in need of books for your kids. What kind?"

"We take anything. I'm working mostly with little kids right now. Hence the paint and glue stuck to me all the time. It's just that they come to us with so little, except for the number of problems."

"Books are an excellent escape." He drank his coffee and thought about where he could get books for her. His mother would know. She knew the ins and outs of many things when it came to charity. "What was your favorite book at that age?"

"*The Little Engine That Could.*"

Even as a child she was prepared to save other children and make a difference. "Then I guess we'll have to start with that one, won't we?"

"Who are you?" she asked, her voice so quiet it was nearly a whisper.

"*The hoper of far-flung hopes and the dreamer of improbable dreams.*"

She leaned forward and propped her chin in her hand. He became uneasy beneath her scrutiny, so he stood. "I have to get going. I have rehearsal."

"So you're an actor."

He nodded. "Until next time."

"Wait. What are you rehearsing?"

"*A Christmas Carol.* I'm Scrooge's nephew, Fred." Free left the coffee shop with a great sense of accomplishment. Not only had Samantha talked with him and asked him to sit with her, she'd told him about herself. Even he knew that if she wasn't interested in him at all, she wouldn't have bothered.

SAMANTHA FINISHED HER COFFEE AND DROVE TO her parents' house in Lake Forest. The drive home always did something strange to her. She found comfort in the sights, but that nagging feeling still pulled at her. She hated feeling this way. It was time to put her foot down and be her own person.

Instead of leaving her car parked in the circle drive, she pulled in near the garage to make it easier for her parents to put the car away. It wouldn't be coming back to the city with her. She let herself into the house and called, "Mom?"

"In here, honey."

She followed her mom's voice to the kitchen. She found it funny that her mom so often sat in the room, because Sam couldn't remember a time her mother ever cooked.

"Hi, Mom." Sam walked through the room and kissed her mom on the cheek.

Vanessa closed the book she had on the table and removed her reading glasses. "What are you doing home? We didn't expect to see you until the holidays after finals."

Her mom acted like the drive from the city took days. She came home occasionally on the weekends just to visit, but her mom seemed to forget that.

"I've made some decisions and I want to talk to you and Dad about them."

"Your father's not home yet. I don't know when he will be. Why don't you stay for dinner and wait with me?"

"I can't. I have studying to do." She sat across from her mom. Nerves roiled and the coffee in her stomach splashed uneasily. "I'm leaving my car here."

"Is there something wrong with it? I can call the mechanic now." Vanessa reached for her phone.

"No, Mom. It's fine. It's just…I hate driving that expensive car when I'm working with people who aren't sure where their next meal is coming from. I have twenty kids in the shelter right now who can't count on Christmas."

"Sweetheart, if you need a donation for your work, just ask. You don't need to make some noble gesture. We'd be happy to help."

Sam sighed. "It's not about donations, Mom. It's about who I am. I need to stand on my own, to make my own life. I can't do that if I'm driving your car and living in the apartment you pay for."

"That's ridiculous. Your father and I have worked hard to provide you with a good life. You can do whatever you want with your life, but you don't have to throw away all of the advantages we gave you."

Sam pinched the bridge of her nose. "I'm not

throwing away the advantages you've given me. I'm using my education to get the career I want. I just don't feel right flaunting my family's money in front of people who have nothing."

Her mother reached out and took her hand. "Money isn't evil."

"I know that. But it clouds things. That car is an invitation for trouble in some of the neighborhoods I travel."

Vanessa sighed. "So you'll keep your apartment then? That can't possibly cause trouble."

"I'll stay at least through graduation, when I can get a job. Then I don't know."

"Your father and I feel so much better with you in an apartment with a doorman. It seems safer." She patted the hand she held. "We worry about you."

"I'm a big girl. I need to be able to take care of myself."

"We both know your father isn't going to like this, so I hope you're prepared for a fight."

The words weren't lost on Sam. She'd have to fight her dad, but her mom was in her corner.

"Thanks, Mom."

"Now, tell me more about these kids who have you all worked up."

Sam went to the stove and started to boil some water for tea. "The shelter does amazing work. Women leave horrible conditions to come to us. They've been beaten down, physically and emotionally, yet they somehow find the courage to run. But it seems like the run itself is all they had energy for. So many of them are still lost when they arrive. They don't know who they are anymore, if they ever did."

"What exactly do you do?" Her mom had shifted so her complete attention was on Sam.

Sam loved that about her mom. No matter what they talked about, Vanessa always gave her total focus. As a teen, she resented it because she felt like she could never get away with anything, but after seeing how other people lived, she'd grown to appreciate it.

"Right now, I mostly play with kids and talk to them. The hours I put in at the shelter work toward my degree. Once I graduate, I don't know that they'll have a paying position for me. In fact, I doubt it. I'll have to look somewhere else, but right now, I can't imagine not being there, so I might continue to volunteer." She walked around the kitchen and pulled out teacups and tea bags while she waited for the water to boil.

"But if you had your degree," her mom continued, "what could you hope to do for these women and their children?"

"I hope to help them realize there is life after abuse. That not everyone is out to hurt them. That they can be valuable members of society. That they can raise their children to have a better life." As she spoke, tears pricked the backs of her eyes and her throat thickened. She thought of the women she saw with such hollow looks in their eyes and her heart went out to them, especially because she knew so many would return to their old lives.

The kettle whistled and Sam turned her attention to the tea. Her mom came up next to her and put an arm around her shoulder.

"I'm proud of you. I had my doubts when you declared your major and told us you wanted to be a social worker."

"Why?" She knew her dad hadn't loved her decision, but her mom never let on.

"I knew you would excel at it. You're empathetic and love to help people. But you're so softhearted that I worried that it would tear you apart. Social work isn't for the faint of heart. But seeing you now, hearing the conviction in your voice, I'm not sure what to think."

Sam poured water into the waiting teacups and handed one to her mom. They sat back down at the breakfast nook. "I've enjoyed the work I've done at other locations, but this one just feels right. I don't know how to explain it. When I first walked in, I thought it would be horrible. I mean, what do I know about abused women and kids?"

She looked around the kitchen that was nothing short of lavish with its stainless steel appliances and marble counters. Life here had been easy. She never had to worry about anything.

"What changed?"

What *had* changed? At what point did walking through the doors of the Hope Center become normal for her? "I don't know." She thought back and knew. It had been Alex. The girl had been only eight when she and her mother came to the shelter.

Because she didn't have her degree, Sam was told she was there to offer support not counseling. She could play with the children or aid with homework, help women with their résumés or filling out job applications. During a spur-of-the-moment art project with a few kids, Alex drew a picture and then blurted out that her mother's boyfriend had molested her.

Sam had frozen, knowing she wasn't supposed to counsel the child, but Alex had looked up with her big brown eyes needing some reassurance. Sam simply said, "That was wrong and it wasn't your fault."

Then she'd taken Alex to her supervisor and together with Alex's mom, they got the details. Alex hadn't told her mom out of fear of retribution from the boyfriend.

"Where did you just go?" Sam's mom asked, pulling her from her thoughts.

"I was thinking about when things changed for me at the Hope Center. It was actually a who. I helped a little girl and her mom. They had a terrible story and they trusted me to help."

Sam called a ride share to get her back to the city. As she and her mom drank their tea, she filled her mom in on school and friends. Before long, the car arrived.

Her mom stood. "Are you sure you won't reconsider? It's just a car. We could probably talk your dad into trading it for something less…"

Sam shook her head. "It's okay, Mom. I live near the el stop and there are always buses running. I can get anywhere I need to with very little hassle. The car is more trouble than it's worth most of the time. Trying to find parking is horrible, and then there's rush hour on the expressway."

"If you're sure."

"I am. This will be a good experience for all of us." She made a scissor motion with her fingers. "Cut those apron strings a little."

Her mom smiled and pulled her into a hug. "You can try to cut away all you want, but I'm holding on."

"Thanks."

The ride back to the city felt like it took forever. By the time she walked through her front door, she was exhausted. She collapsed on her couch with her laptop so she could study. Instead, she Googled "Doctor Who tenth doctor." *Cute. Dorky, but cute.* Much like her actor friend. She immediately recognized the clothes she'd seen earlier in the day. His face was different, of course, but he'd nailed the costume.

She wondered how he chose the characters to dress up as. And why? Even more important, what was his name?

Her homework sat untouched as she started Netflix and searched for *Doctor Who.* Maybe watching might give her some insight into who this guy was.

~

FREE WALKED INTO HIS CHILDHOOD HOME AND yelled, "I'm home."

"What's with the yelling?" his mom called from the living room.

Free left his jacket in the foyer and walked into the living room, where his mother was entertaining some guests. Whoops. "Sorry, Mom. I didn't know you had people over."

She rose from her seat and kissed his cheek. "You might be more aware of what happens around here if you visited more often. How are you?"

"I'm fine. I wanted to drop off these." He pulled the tickets for opening night from his pocket.

"Oh, lovely." She turned to her friends. "My son, Humphrey, is starring in *A Christmas Carol.*"

"I'm not starring. I'm Fred."

She poked his arm. "Still a major role. It's not like you're a caroler."

"They couldn't cast me as a caroler. I can't sing for sh—anything."

His mom shot him a sharp look. Although Amelia Mitchell cursed on occasion, she would never stand for it with company in the house. "Um, is Dad around?"

"In his study, as always."

He waved to his mother's friends. "Nice to see you all." Then he ducked back through the foyer to the other end of the house to see his dad.

Entering his dad's study was like stepping back in time. Free remembered being young, maybe six, and sneaking in here and sitting under the desk to listen to his father work. Anthony Mitchell always seemed so important. He had phone calls to make and meetings to attend.

In a way, none of that had changed. His father was a major player in investment banking, but now it didn't seem so mysterious. Free understood the business, so it removed some of the magic. "Hey, Dad."

"Humphrey, what are you doing here?"

"Jeez, can't a guy just visit his parents without having a reason?"

"At twenty-two? No. Sons tend to come home when they want something."

"Well, I wanted to talk to Mom, but she's busy."

"Anything I can help with?"

His dad help with charity? Not likely. "No, but did you see that Tritec is poised to take over Omnibyte?"

"Who are Tritec and Omnibyte?" Even as he asked, his dad was pulling up company information on his computer.

"They're both relatively small tech firms, but together, they can be in a position to become major players."

"Where did you hear about this?"

"I read. You have the *Wall Street Journal* delivered to my apartment even though I can access it online." Free took a seat in the oversized leather chair across from his father.

"I saw nothing about this."

"You would've overlooked them. They haven't made a big enough splash for most people to notice. But I've been watching. Tritec just got an influx of new investors, and it looks like they're prepared to announce something big before attempting a takeover."

His dad didn't respond. He was absorbed in reading whatever was on the screen in front of him. Free knew better than to keep talking.

"Hmm," his dad grunted.

Free had become an expert in deciphering his father's noises. This type of grunt meant he was considering the options. After a few minutes of typing on the computer and taking notes on a legal pad, his dad looked up. "Looks promising. I'll get someone on it."

Free wished that someone could be him. His dad gave a pile of folders on his desk a little shove.

"Take a look at these. See what you think."

Free reached over and pulled the stack onto his lap. The files contained financials on various companies that his dad must've been considering investing in.

"Can I take these with me?"

His dad nodded. Ever since last summer, his dad occasionally gave him some research to do even though he wasn't officially on staff yet. He needed to prove himself because other guys would be out to get him from day one. He was the boss's son, so he knew the target on his back would last until he'd proven he was good enough to be a banker.

His dad had no doubts, which made him feel better, but he remembered the tough time Cary had when he started. Other guys sabotaged his every move. It was part of what led to Cary's depression and overeating. Cary had a hard time reconciling the ease with which he interacted with clients with the issues he'd had with colleagues.

"When do you need them back?"

"Yesterday?"

"I have class tomorrow and then rehearsal, but I can have the analysis done the following morning."

"Rehearsal?"

"*A Christmas Carol*. I left tickets with Mom in case you want to come see it." He knew his dad wouldn't. Theater wasn't his thing. He'd indulged Free's mom and her love of acting over the years and he tolerated it in Free, but he had zero interest in watching.

"Why didn't Cary come with you today?"

Free shrugged. He hadn't even asked Cary if he wanted to. "Don't you see him at work?"

"Sometimes. I have better things to do than check in on every employee."

"How long do you think Mom's friends are going to be here?"

His dad threw up his hands. "I never know. I stay out of the way so they don't try to rope me in to any plan they're hatching."

"What are they doing?"

"To tell you the truth, I have no idea. You know your mother. She's part of so many groups and organizations, who can keep track? I thought today might be book club. If it is, they should be done soon. Unless…"

"Unless what?"

"Did they have a bottle of wine open?"

"Not that I saw."

He dad laughed. "Then they're probably wrapping up. Every now and again, they read something sad and then they open wine. They drink and cry over imaginary people."

A soft knock sounded at the office door and then it swung open. Amelia strode in. "How are my boys?"

"Good meeting?" his dad asked.

"Wonderful." She turned her attention to Free. "Why are you really here?"

"I came to ask you about a charity thing."

Amelia clapped. "I love a new project. What are you considering?"

Free stood. "Let's go to the other room so Dad can finish his work."

Amelia led the way out of the office. His dad mouthed a thank-you to Free as they left.

"I met this girl."

Amelia spun and gripped his arm. "That's wonderful. What's her name? How long have you been seeing her? When will you bring her by?"

"We aren't dating. I just met her at the coffee shop, and she was telling me about a shelter she works at and how the kids there need books."

She looped her arm around his and tugged him toward the kitchen. "A book drive. I love a good book drive. What's the shelter?"

"I actually don't know. She didn't give me the name, but I'll probably see her tomorrow. I can get it then."

"I'll call the girls tonight. It's the perfect time for a book drive. People are out for holiday shopping. What's it take to grab a book and drop it in a donation bin? We'll have a library for your girl by the first of the year."

His girl? Not even close. His mom's positive disposition rubbed off on him, though. She'd always had the ability to make him believe in the improbable. Hearing his mom develop a plan to impress a girl made him believe he might really have a chance with Samantha.

CHAPTER THREE

Samantha found herself standing in the coffee shop waiting for whatever his name was. How ridiculous was it that she liked a guy but didn't even know his name? She didn't wait for guys; it wasn't her style. But she had a feeling he'd be coming to get his usual coffee before rushing out to rehearsal.

Interesting that he drank boring old black coffee. He was such a colorful, unique guy in his costumes that it seemed he should have a more complicated coffee order.

The door opened and in he came, carrying a plastic bag. He wore a fedora and a leather jacket instead of his longer overcoat. He smiled a cocky grin and then she realized that he was Indiana Jones.

"You're here."

He tipped his hat. *"I'm like a bad penny. I always turn up."* He stepped toward the counter to order.

"Wait." She laid a hand on his arm and then realized that was more personal than they'd been and snatched her hand back. "We've met and talked a couple of times now, but I still don't know your real name."

He extended a hand to shake. "Humphrey, but my friends call me Free."

"Free," she repeated with a nod and shook his hand.

The name was unusual, but suited him. Old-fashioned, yet the nickname was fresh. "Ready for coffee?"

"As always."

She allowed him to order for her. She liked that he paid attention to her order. Of course he waved off her offer to pay for hers. They sat at a table and he slid the plastic bag over to her. "What's this?"

"Open it."

Inside the bag, she found five copies of *The Little Engine That Could*. Her throat tightened.

"You said there were kids, as in more than one, but I didn't know how many. I figured five would be a good number to start with."

"You bought me books?" The words barely squeezed out.

"What's the name of the shelter you work at?"

The question had her looking up sharply. "Why?"

"My mother is always looking for a cause and I told her about you needing books. When I talked to her yesterday, she was ready to start working on a book drive. But I didn't know the name of your shelter, so I couldn't tell her."

Sam studied his face.

"Is it a secret or something?"

"Not really." She hesitated. "The thing is, the

women come to us for shelter and safety. So while the name isn't a secret, we don't advertise where to find us."

His face filled with confusion. "Then how do the women find you?"

"Word of mouth, social services, churches."

"You don't have to tell me anything. I can give you my mom's number and you can explain to her."

"No. I'm overreacting. It's called the Hope Center."

"Good name." He drank another sip. "I have to get going to rehearsal."

"Before you go, can you tell me why you're dressed in a different costume every time I see you? This is obviously not *A Christmas Carol*."

He pressed his lips together. "Last summer, my brother was warned by his doctor to lose weight or he'd end up having a stroke. He was embarrassed to go to a gym because he felt like everyone stared. I volunteered to go with him and dress up in costume to draw attention away from him." He lifted a shoulder as if it was no big deal.

Sam's heart gave a little lurch. She'd known after that first chance meeting that he was a sweet guy, albeit a little weird. This confirmed it. "That's really cool of you."

"He's my big brother." He stood to leave.

She reached into her bag, grabbed a scrap of paper, and scribbled on it. "Here's my number. You can pass it on to your mom or whatever." She sincerely hoped the "whatever" would include him calling her for a date.

He tucked it into his pocket. "See you next week?"

"Definitely." Sam grabbed her phone and snapped another picture of him.

"What was that for?"

She didn't know why she took the photo. But she'd looked at the one of him as Sherlock Holmes more than a few times since they first spoke. "I've never met Indiana Jones before. My friends will never believe me."

"Had I known you wanted a photo op, I would've pulled out my whip."

She laughed, sure he was kidding, but he swept aside his jacket and unfurled a whip. Her jaw dropped. He took his costumes seriously.

"Now I'm ready for a picture." He winked at her.

She took another photo. This time, he posed with the whip over his head and he gave her that same cocky grin he had when he came in. "Thanks."

"Any time."

She watched as he rolled up his whip and left the shop. Then she texted the picture to Jess.

Isn't that the same guy who was Sherlock Holmes?

Yep.

Of course, then her phone rang. Jess would want details, not a text. "Hi."

"I thought we agreed you wouldn't encourage the weirdos."

"He's not a weirdo. I got the whole story and it's sweet."

"I can't wait to hear this."

"His name is Free, short for Humphrey. He dresses in costume to help his brother. His brother needs to work out and is embarrassed when people stare at him, so Free dresses up to take the attention off his brother. Isn't that sweet?" She slipped a copy of *The Little Engine That Could* from the bag.

"Still sounds weird."

"When we talked the other day, I mentioned that we need books at the shelter. He asked me what my favorite book is and today he showed up with five copies for me to take to the shelter for the kids."

"What's his angle?"

"What?"

"You just met this guy, this weird guy who plays dress-up, and he's bringing you presents. What does he want?"

Sam stared at the glossy cover of the book. "Why does he have to have an angle? Can't he just like me?"

"Sure he can. You're totally lovable, but I'm suspicious by nature."

Jess's words made her think. Could Free have ulterior motives?

"You got awful quiet. What aren't you saying?"

"Nothing. I was thinking about whether Free might be after something. But I've got nothing. He's nice guy. I like him." She put the book back in the bag. "And I hope he calls me and asks me out."

"Aw, man, you gave him your number?"

Sam imagined Jess's eyes rolling back in her head making her looked possessed. "Yes. He said his mom might be interested in doing a book drive for the shelter, so I gave him my number to pass on to her."

"If it was just about a donation, why not give the shelter's number?"

"He offered to give me his mom's number, but I decided he could have mine. Plus, like I said, I'm hoping he'll take the hint and call me."

Jess's sigh came rolling over the line. She'd known Jess since freshman year. They were roommates and Jess had constantly teased her about being too naïve about everything. She wasn't naïve; she chose to see the good in people.

"I'm fine, Jess."

"I want to meet this guy. Check him out myself."

"Believe it or not, I'm capable of going out on a date without your approval."

"And look how those have turned out."

"Shut up." She stood and bundled up for her walk to the el. "Besides, he might not even call me."

"We'll see. Drinks tomorrow night?"

"If I get my homework done, sure. Call me in the afternoon."

FREE HAD BEEN RESTLESS SINCE HE LEFT SAMANTHA the previous afternoon. The little bits of time with her at the coffee shop had become his favorite parts of the week, but he wanted more. So he called the one guy who could help him. Hunter.

He'd called and woken Hunter up this morning

and made lunch plans. Now he sat in his car outside the sub shop waiting. As usual.

Free ran through his lines for extra practice while he waited. Hunter tapped on the window as he walked by, not waiting for Free to get out of his car.

Inside the restaurant, Hunter pointed at Free's hat. "Didn't we outgrow that stuff about fifteen years ago?"

Free shrugged. "It's warm."

"So, what's wrong?"

"Who said anything was wrong?"

"You called me at five thirty this morning to make lunch plans. What's her name?"

Free pulled off his hat, bunching the pom-poms in his fist, and blew out a breath. He hated that Hunter knew him so well. "Let's order first."

"I knew it."

They placed their orders for foot-long Italian subs, extra dressing. They grabbed a booth and as they unwrapped their sandwiches, Hunter said, "Shoot."

Without looking up from his food, Free said, "There's this girl, Samantha."

"Knew it," Hunter said with a smirk.

"I met her at the coffee shop near the gym where I meet Cary."

"Have you talked to her yet?"

"Yeah. A couple of times." He bit into his sandwich. "I even bought her a cup of coffee."

"Wait a minute. You said you met her after the gym?"

Free nodded.

"So you were wearing one of your costumes."

"That's just it. Every time I've seen her, I've been coming from the gym. She's only seen me in costume."

"Hmm…I don't know if it's a positive or negative. She's seen you at your craziest: plus. If she's not weirded out by it: negative."

Free shrugged. "I think she likes it. Even before I talked to her, I saw her watching me, like waiting to see how I'd be dressed. The last time, she asked to take my picture."

"Are you sure she's not a crazy?"

"She seems normal. She's studying to be a social worker, so she's in the area every day for volunteer work at some shelter."

"So what's the problem?"

"She's only seen me in costume at the coffee shop. How do I move past that?"

"That's your problem? Easy—ask her out."

"Easy for you maybe." Free picked at the lettuce on his sandwich.

Hunter set down his half-eaten sub and wiped his hands on a napkin. "When will you see her again?"

Free shrugged.

"Next time, tell her that although you like your brief meetings, you'd like to extend your time with her. Ask her if she's free for dinner."

"Just like that? Tell her I want to go out with her?" He'd asked girls out before and it was definitely a hit-or-miss thing. Usually miss.

"Yeah. Did you think there was some magic to it? I just ask. She has no way of knowing how you feel unless you tell her. Maybe she's thinking you're a strange guy who likes to chat over coffee.

I've seen you flirt. You can't throw out a line to save your life. You need the direct approach." Hunter dove back into his sandwich. "The worst that happens is that she says no."

He swallowed hard. The thought of being rejected by Samantha stung. He wasn't ready to lose their short conversations. "Then what?"

"If you really want her, you try again. Some women appreciate persistence."

"And some would call you a stalker."

Hunter laughed. "Hopefully, you get the hint before that point."

Free didn't tell Hunter that he had Samantha's phone number, because Hunter would pressure him to use it now. Free wasn't sure if he'd have better luck over the phone or in person.

They finished their lunches and discussed more about New Year's Eve. Hunter seemed to be quietly accepting that he couldn't have the blowout he wanted because both Free and Adam were working on getting dates. As ridiculous as the deal seemed, Hunter had offered it. Not having an apartment full of strangers to wade through might be worth putting himself out there and asking Samantha for a date.

Last year's party had been "epic" in Hunter's words, but Free had been miserable. He hardly knew anyone and it was so loud, conversation had been impossible. He wanted this year to be different.

They separated after lunch and Free sat in his car again, this time holding his phone and the scrap of paper with Samantha's number. He flipped the paper over in his fingers and attempted to gather the courage Hunter spoke so flippantly about.

Screw it. Hunter had said to just ask.

So Free sent a text, carefully crafting it so he wouldn't come off like a stalker.

Hi, Samantha, it's Free—I know you gave me your number for my mom, but I was wondering if you might be interested in going out tomorrow night. Dinner or drinks, or a movie if you prefer.

When he was finally content that it was okay, he hit SEND and waited. After staring at his phone for five minutes, he gave up, sensing defeat. She would probably avoid the coffee shop now in order to dodge him.

He pulled out of the lot and drove back to school. Although he didn't have class this afternoon, he could get some studying in before rehearsal. As he walked through the doors to the library, his phone buzzed.

I'd love to.

His heart lurched into his throat. She hadn't dodged him. She wanted to go out on a date. He couldn't believe his eyes.

After checking the number to make sure it was, in fact, from Samantha, he responded: **Brilliant!**

She wouldn't get the *Doctor Who* reference, but it was confident. Then he added, **I'll call you tomorrow and we'll figure out details.**

Sitting down in a study nook, he realized that he wouldn't be focusing on books at all. His brain raced with ideas for dates. He needed it to be perfect.

CHAPTER FOUR

Sam stood in front of the mirror and scooped her hair up, then let it fall again around her shoulders. She turned from side to side. Glancing down at her jeans, she had no idea if she was dressed okay for her date with Free. He'd said to dress casual, but then added something about wearing clothes she wouldn't care about getting messy. He wouldn't tell her what the date entailed, though.

He seemed really nervous the couple of times they talked, so she didn't press him. She was happy that he'd used her number to ask her out. When they left each other at the coffee shop, she'd been worried that he wasn't going to call. With a quick swipe of lip gloss, she decided that her outfit would have to do. If Free showed up wearing something fancier, she could change.

The phone rang, and the doorman let her know Free was here. She told him to send Free up. She snapped a hair tie on her wrist in case she needed to put her hair up later and waited nervously by the door. She couldn't remember the last time she'd been this anxious over a date.

Maybe it was because Free seemed so different from the guys she usually dated. While Jess had been right in thinking she sometimes chose guys who would make her dad crazy, they had mostly been of the bad boy variety. Free didn't fit that mold at all. Although she didn't know much about him, she knew he was sweet.

Any guy who would dress up in crazy costumes to help his brother had to be nice. And given the costumes he'd chosen, he must've been a geek of the highest order. He dressed as characters she'd barely heard of.

When the elevator dinged, she opened her door to look for him. She didn't know what she'd expected, but he managed to surprise her. He got off the elevator carrying a bouquet of roses. From what she could see under his plain jacket, he appeared to be wearing normal jeans, which didn't tell her much because he also wore the same red Converses he'd worn when he was Doctor Who.

He looked up and when their eyes met, his face broke into a wide smile. "Hi."

"Hi. I hope you didn't have a hard time finding the place."

"Nope. Your directions were excellent. I actually don't live too far from here." He held out the bouquet. "These are for you."

She accepted them and brought them to her face for a deep sniff. "Thank you. They're beautiful." She took a step back into her apartment. "Come in."

He followed her and closed the door behind him.

"I'll put these in water." As she moved around the kitchen, she continued to talk. "You still haven't said where we're going, so I hope I'm dressed okay."

He strode into the kitchen with his jacket open. He, too, wore a T-shirt with his jeans. His dark blue T-shirt read HERMITS UNITE! in white letters.

"Interesting shirt. Are you sure it's all right to leave your cave to be out in public?"

He ran a hand over the front of his shirt. "Uh, it's another Doctor Who reference."

She smiled at that. Even not in costume, he wore his geekhood. "Speaking of which, I watched a few episodes of the tenth doctor. You were quoting him."

"Huh?"

"When we talked about books. You said something like books are the best weapons. I thought it was cool at the time, but then I learned you stole the line from *Doctor Who*."

He blushed but took a step closer to her. "I tend to do that—use lines from the character I'm portraying. It's the actor in me."

"Is that all?"

"No. It also makes things easier when I'm nervous. If I use someone else's words, I won't embarrass myself."

"Interesting tactic. I might have to give it a try."

He laughed. "You? I can't imagine you ever get nervous."

"Maybe I'm a better actor than you are." The air between them filled with tension, but it was good. She drew nearer to him. "For instance, I'm extremely nervous right now."

"Why?" His voice had dropped to a lower register, and it was sexy as hell.

"Because I want tonight to be good, and first dates tend to suck."

"I'll do my level best to make sure it doesn't."

She stood close enough that she watched his pulse thump in his neck. She had the urge to kiss him to see if his pulse would spike, but part of her feared it would scare him away.

She licked her lips, tasting her strawberry gloss, and asked, "Ready to go?"

He stepped back and swept out an arm. "*As you wish.*"

She pointed at him. "I know that one. *Princess Bride*, right?"

"Very good."

"You won't need quotes tonight. You already got me on a date. No need to be nervous." She reached into the closet and tugged her coat off a hanger.

"Easier said than done."

"I always thought that for a guy, asking was the hardest part."

"True, it only takes about *twenty seconds of insane courage.*"

"Ha! I know that one too. *We Bought a Zoo*. Don't you think it's a little weird that you can pull out quotes throughout a conversation like it's nothing?"

He took her coat and held it open for her to slide into. "*We're all pretty bizarre. Some of us are just better at hiding it, that's all.*"

She turned, still standing close enough to brush against him as she pulled her coat closed. She stared and tried to decide whether that was another quote.

He slowly slid his hands under her hair and freed it from where it had been trapped under her collar. In doing so, he was even closer. She smelled his cologne and wanted to bury her nose in his neck. His thumbs caressed her neck and he leaned close to her ear. *"The Breakfast Club."*

His breath on her ear sent a *zing* through her body. Something about his quiet mannerisms made her want to rub up against him. She inhaled deeply, and her boobs brushed his chest.

"We better leave, or we'll be late." He took a step away from her.

"Hmm…if it's something we'll be late for, then it's not just dinner. At least not someplace casual enough for T-shirts and jeans. Any other clues?"

"Nope."

Then he surprised her by reaching out to hold her hand. It was a simple thing, but as her palm slid against his, another *zing* zipped through her, up her arm, down her torso, and straight to her girly parts.

They got into his car—a modest Honda—and he drove to Halsted. She had no idea where he was taking her until she saw the theater. "Are we going to Blue Man Group?"

He twitched a little at her question. "Yeah. Is that okay? I mean, unless you've seen it recently, it's still a great time. They change it up."

She practically danced in her seat. "No. I mean,

yeah, it's okay. I've always wanted to see it, but my friends never wanted to go."

His shoulders relaxed and he smiled. She put her hand over his on top of the gear lever. "Stop being nervous. Even if I'd seen it yesterday, I wouldn't have said anything. It would be a really bitchy move to ruin something that you obviously put thought into."

"Yeah, well…"

"What kind of girls have you dated that this was a real concern?" Although she asked the question rhetorically, part of her wanted the answer.

He pulled into a lot, paid for parking, then walked around to the passenger side to meet her. Definitely a sweet guy.

Inside the dark theater lobby, he led the way. The place was crowded and although he turned to make sure she was close, the press of people worried her. Then he reached back and grabbed her hand. She liked the connection. He led her down near the front and handed her some plastic.

"What is this?"

"We're in the poncho seats. Trust me, wear it." He unfolded his poncho and slipped it on, so she did the same.

They settled in their seats, and nerves rattled through her. How gross was this going to be that they needed ponchos? Maybe she misunderstood what the show was.

As if sensing her fear, Free leaned close and said, "Trust me. It's fun."

And he was right. The show was awesome. Paint splattering, marshmallows flying, drums beating. It was excellent. She laughed so hard she'd cried. When she saw Free laughing with her, she knew she was experiencing the best first date of her life.

FREE COULDN'T REMEMBER A TIME HE'D LAUGHED so hard with a girl. With Adam and Hunter? Sure. But never on a date. He didn't even know why he'd thought Blue Man Group would be a good choice for Samantha, but he was glad he got the tickets. When the show ended, they fought their way out into the cold night air. After getting in the car, he asked Sam where she wanted to go for dinner.

"Whatever. It doesn't matter."

"Well, given the way we're dressed, we need to stick with something casual. Are you sure you don't have a preference?"

"Nope. I'm safe in your hands."

Satisfaction warmed him at her words. He'd known he hit the mark when he caught her laughing throughout the show, but hearing her acknowledge it was even better. Who needed to throw out a line when the direct approach worked? Hunter was on to something here.

He drove down the street and over to Clark where they could find a bar that served food.

Unfortunately, he was not a bar aficionado and the one he chose had crappy food. At least the beer was okay. As long as they ordered bottled beer. But none of that seemed to matter to Samantha. They laughed and joked about school and parents and friends. Before he knew it, it was after midnight.

"I should probably get you home." What he really wanted more than anything was to go home with her, but he wasn't smooth enough to nab that invitation on a first date. It was important to know your limitations.

She released a loud yawn and quickly slapped a hand over her mouth. "I'm so sorry. That had nothing to do with the quality of our date. I was up really early this morning."

He helped her into her coat and drove her home. On the drive, his mind raced. Should he park and walk her in? Should he pull up and let her out? What about a kiss? He definitely wanted a kiss. His car was not made for a lingering goodnight kiss. Reaching across the console left too much space.

Park. Definitely park. He pulled into a metered spot on the street.

"You don't have to park."

Shit. She had a good time. Didn't she want him to kiss her?

"I mean, you've paid for our entire evening. It seems silly to pay for parking for a few minutes' walk up to my door."

"It's worth the extra couple of bucks to walk you in." He paid the meter and opened her door to help her out.

They walked toward the front entrance and she suddenly spun around. "I don't sleep with guys on the first date."

"Okay. I didn't have that expectation."

She smiled and looped her arm around his. "I

like that you're a gentleman who opens doors and walks me in. A lot of guys don't do that."

"My mother taught me and my brother that there was a certain way to treat women. If we aren't willing to put in the little bit of extra work, we don't deserve the girl." His mom's words echoed in his head every time he was on a date.

As they walked through the small lobby, Samantha waved at the doorman. She pressed the elevator button and leaned against the wall. "I had a really good time tonight."

"So did I." The elevator arrived and with each climbing floor, Free's heart rate kicked up as self-doubt reared its head.

On her floor she stepped out and he followed her to her door. He swallowed hard, determined not to screw this up, and reached for her hand. "Will I see you at the coffee shop this week?"

"I'll be looking for you."

"I'd like to take you on another date."

"I would like that very much." She spoke quietly and her eyes focused on his.

He stared into her light brown eyes and tried to read them. She tugged him closer with a hand bunched in his jacket. "Do you have a movie quote for this moment?"

His mind scrambled through a thousand words he could use, but his concentration was on her soft pink lips. He nodded slowly. "Have you ever seen *Bull Durham*?"

She shook her head.

"I believe in long, slow, deep, soft, wet kisses that last three days."

She nodded and twined her arms around his neck. "That one definitely works."

He lowered his head and their mouths met. Soft and slow, lips interlocking, then Free tilted his head a little more and teased her lips open with his tongue. She tasted like strawberries. She sucked on his tongue and he felt it all the way down to his dick. He pressed her up against the wall, enjoying the softness of her body. He couldn't feel much through the layers of clothes, but his hands gripped her hips and held her close.

By the time they separated, they were both breathless. Her chest rose and fell in time with his. *"You should be kissed and often, and by someone who knows how."* He paused before stepping away from her. *"Gone with the Wind."*

A slow smile crept onto her face. "I think you have that covered."

She licked her lips and the sight of her wet tongue made him want to do much more than kiss her.

"Monday at the coffee shop?" she asked, her breathing still irregular.

"I'll be there." He took another step back, this time allowing enough distance for them both to catch a deep breath. "Can I call you tomorrow?"

"I'd like that."

He waited in the hall until she went into her apartment and locked the door. He might've been walking a little funny on the way to the elevator because his dick was hard, but that kiss had been well worth any amount of discomfort. It made him wish he'd spoken to Samantha sooner than he had.

The holidays were quickly approaching and they didn't know each other well enough to do the family thing, but that meant he might not see much of her. They would just have to squeeze in as much time as possible around family commitments. He immediately began cataloguing what he needed to attend. Unfortunately, rehearsals were only going to become a bigger part of his life, and for once, he wanted to ignore acting.

CHAPTER FIVE

*S*queezing in time together proved more difficult than Free thought. Although they spoke every day, and texted often, other than their fleeting meetings over coffee, Free hadn't spent any time with Samantha. They were both swamped with end-of-the-semester assignments and work. But at least they'd been able to share some kisses over their coffee. Most days, they preferred that to conversation.

Free had had enough. He texted Sam to see if she would come with him to his rehearsal tonight. Then, they could go out, or stay in, and have some time together. Her response made her sound as excited as he was at the prospect of having more than fifteen minutes together.

Samantha was waiting in line at the coffee shop as usual. He crossed the room and kissed her cheek.

She pulled at the front of his jacket and peered down. "Who are you today?"

He smiled and opened his coat. "Han Solo." He whipped out the blaster from his holster.

"Cute boots. From a distance, I thought maybe a pirate, but the hair's a little wrong."

"No Jack Sparrow for me. Smuggler, pirate, not too different."

"Take off your jacket."

"Why?"

"So I can take a picture to add to my collection."

He did as he was told and she snapped a couple of pictures on her phone.

They ordered their coffee and instead of sitting, took it straight to his car. "So what made you invite me to rehearsal?"

"I want to spend time with you, and the play is going to fill my next two weekends. Then it's the holidays."

"I'm glad you did. I can't wait to see you in action up on the stage."

Although rehearsals were usually laid-back and there were often outsiders watching, Free had never invited anyone to rehearsals. He rarely invited people to come to the actual performances. His mother insisted on coming to every play he'd ever done, but she loved the theater. He was fine performing, but he didn't like people he knew watching.

They got to the small theater a few minutes early, so Free gave Samantha a quick tour and then situated her in the audience. He changed into his costume and did a few warm-ups. He focused on the words he needed to say instead of on the beautiful woman waiting for him.

They ran through the play in one set, with few interruptions from the director. The cast and crew had been at this long enough that they were ready for opening night tomorrow. By the time rehearsal was over, Free wanted nothing more than a shower and a cold drink. Then he thought of Samantha and knew he wanted a whole lot more. He grabbed his bag and went to the audience to look for her.

She sat exactly where he'd left her hours ago. He should've checked on her during the performance.

"Hey," he called as he crossed the row of seats to get to her.

"Oh my God. That was so interesting. I've never seen the behind-the-scenes stuff of a performance before. And you are an excellent Fred. I didn't realize that this was an updated version of the story." She stood and gathered her coat as she spoke.

"The writer thought Dickens was too out of reach for a lot of people, mainly kids, so he wanted to update the story without losing the feel of it."

"Are you done?"

"Yeah. What would you like to do?" He swung his bag over his shoulder. "I'd like to take a shower, if you don't mind. It's been a long day with classes, the gym with Cary, and rehearsal."

She walked down the aisle beside him. Pointing to his bag, she asked, "Do you have clothes in there?"

He nodded.

"How about we go to my place, then? You can shower and change and we can order in some dinner."

"That sounds like an excellent idea." He took her hand as they exited the theater.

On the drive to her apartment, she asked more about his costumes and Cary. They talked about how he decided on his costumes—his favorite characters who had simple clothes. She laughed when he talked about rarely being the Riddler because tights were *not* comfortable.

She surprised him by saying, "Riddler is my favorite villain."

"Why?"

"His disguise might not have been the best, but he always made Batman think. Nothing was simple with him."

He wasn't surprised that intelligence impressed her.

She leaned over and ran a hand along his thigh. His dick twitched in response.

"Would you wear it for me?"

"What?"

"The Riddler costume."

Christ. If she kept moving her hand up his thigh, he'd do anything she asked. "Maybe."

She giggled and told him to park in her spot, which made him wonder about her car. "You don't drive?"

"I can. I have a license and all, but no car right now. Living and working in the city, I found I don't really need one. Public transportation works, and if I'm in a bind, I call a car."

"Did you grow up in the city?"

She hesitated at the elevator before answering. "Lake Forest. How about you?"

She said it like she was embarrassed, as if

coming from a wealthy suburb was a bad thing. "I grew up in the city. North side, until I moved in with Cary for college."

Once they got in the elevator, Samantha stepped close to him and backed him against the wall. She pulled at the front of his jacket until he lowered his mouth to kiss her. Just as he deepened the kiss, the elevator stopped on her floor. Still gripping his jacket, she led him down the hall. She didn't let go until they were at her door and she had to unlock it.

There was something sexy about being led around by a hot girl. Samantha had a plan for their night, and Free wasn't about to interrupt it. She waited for him to walk through the door, then she shut it and grabbed him again. He liked a woman who knew what she wanted.

This time he pressed her against the wall because he enjoyed the feel of her under him. His dick got hard thinking about her naked. He couldn't wait to strip all of her clothes away.

"I missed this," he whispered against her neck.

She sighed as his tongue touched her pulse point. Her hips rocked against him. He wanted to have sex with her, but not down and dirty against her door. He pulled away and couldn't help but notice her shallow breathing. "Why don't you order dinner? I'll take my shower."

"Are you kidding? You're stopping?"

Free braced a hand on the wall near her head. "That was simply my hello-I've-missed-you kiss. We have all night to explore other things."

She ducked under his arm and walked away. Over her shoulder, she said, "I'll hold you to that."

He hung his coat on a hook near the door and picked his bag up from where he'd dropped it during their kiss. His dick was hard and uncomfortable in his tight pants. He couldn't wait to get them off. "Bathroom?" he asked as he reached the kitchen.

"Around the corner on the left. Towels are in the cabinet."

He entered the bathroom, and it was obviously a woman's room. Makeup, perfume, and lotions were scattered across the top of the counter. He picked up the bottle of lotion and sniffed. The scent drove more blood south and his dick throbbed. He twisted the knobs in the shower and stripped while the water warmed.

Inside the tub wasn't any better. Samantha's scent surrounded him in her shampoo and soap. He used a bit of her body wash and cleaned up. He wrapped his hand around his dick and stroked. He needed some release or he wouldn't get through dinner with her. He closed his eyes and imagined her standing in front of him, pulling him closer.

He pumped his hand faster, water sluicing over him. His balls tightened.

A knock at the door made him freeze, which was nearly as painful as being stuffed in his jeans.

"Find everything okay?"

"Uh, yeah. Be out in a minute." Fuck. He slowed his stroke, needing to finish. He hoped she wouldn't come in. She would think he was a total freak with no self-control.

"All right. Holler if you need anything."

What he needed was to come. Her voice shot through him, increasing his need. He pumped his fist quickly and spurted his release. He swallowed the groan that crawled up from his chest. He immediately felt guilty for doing that in Samantha's shower, but at least he wouldn't embarrass himself with her later. Making sure he left no signs of what he'd done, he finished the shower in record time. After drying, he pulled on his clean clothes.

Shoving his costume in his bag, he carried it and his holster to the living room.

SAM LOOKED UP FROM HER SEAT ON THE COUCH AND couldn't help but smile. Free came out of the bathroom with his hair wet and messy, wearing a T-shirt and jeans with his holster slung over his shoulder. He was totally adorkable.

And a huge part of her regretted not getting in the shower with him. He'd sounded surprised when she asked if he had everything he needed and he offered no invitation. Looked like she'd have to put out the invite tonight.

"I ordered Chinese. Hope that's okay with you."

"I'm starving, so you could feed me just about anything right now and I'd be happy." He dropped his bag next to the couch and balanced the holster on top. He sat down beside her, stretching his legs into her space. "How was your week?"

"Okay, I guess."

He leaned forward, bracing his elbow on his leg. "What's wrong?"

She hadn't thought she let any of her depression slip, but Free managed to catch it. "It's a sad time of year."

"The holidays?"

"Yeah." She quickly waved her hand. "Not for me. For the women and kids in the shelter. They don't have much to look forward to."

"I bet it's hard."

"The thing is, the kids, the women, they put on this brave face, like none of it matters. To a certain degree, I understand. For some of them, the lack of certainty about their lives is better than the violence they left. It's their shot at freedom. But to have nothing…" Her throat tightened every time she thought about it.

"They have you and the others at the shelter for support."

"Yeah, I know." She still questioned how much good she was really doing. She wasn't sure how well she could relate to these women. "We arranged with a local YMCA to do a giving tree. You know, where the women write down what gift they'd like to get for Christmas? Then anonymous donors grab a tag from the tree and buy that gift."

"So they'll have something on Christmas."

"But they asked for things like dress shoes for work or cleaning supplies for their apartment. A new rug because the floor is cold."

"Maybe the donors will get them something special in addition to the necessities."

She hoped so. Although she didn't believe that the holidays required big, expensive gifts, she'd never gone without and couldn't imagine Christmas being just another day.

Free reached out and slid her hair away from her face. His finger stroked her cheek. "You can only do what you can. Have you talked to my mom?"

Sam nodded slowly, unwilling to break the contact with his hand. "I actually had her talk to the director so they can hash out the details. She sounded nice. Your mom."

"She is."

"This conversation is pretty depressing. Let's talk about something else until our food gets here."

His fingers trailed over her jaw and down her neck. Anticipation shot through her.

"I can think of other things we can do besides talk."

"But then we'll get interrupted."

He leaned forward and kissed her lightly. As soon as their lips met, she wanted more. More of what she stole in the elevator. Definitely more of what he'd given pressed up against her door. She wanted more of him.

With a gentle hand on his chest, she pushed. "Tell me about your dad."

"Huh?" His gaze was unfocused.

She scooted back on the couch to gain some distance and perspective. For days they'd been talking a lot, but mostly about her. He revealed very little about himself. "You don't talk much about your family. Except Cary. I almost feel like I know him. What about your parents?"

He shook his head as if to clear it and turned his body to sit straight. "My mom's an actress, or at least she used to be. She's still involved with the theater as much as she can, but she doesn't audition anymore. My dad's an investment banker. He has his own firm."

"And Cary works with him?"

"Yeah. Cary's his right hand. As soon as Cary graduated from college, he started bringing in clients. He's got a way with people. Everyone likes him."

Sam felt the undercurrent of what Free wasn't saying. Everyone liked Cary, not him. Her bell rang and she jumped up. "I think the best thing about living in the city is getting whatever kind of food you want delivered."

She went to the door and paid the delivery guy. When she turned, Free was right behind her.

"I would've paid for dinner."

"No big deal. You can get it next time." The words slipped easily from her mouth. Although they'd only been on one date, she felt a connection to him. They hadn't had a serious conversation about exclusivity, but ever since their date, she hadn't thought about anyone else.

She handed the bag to Free. "If you take this to the living room, I'll get us some pop to drink. Sorry, I don't have anything else, unless you want water."

"Pop is good."

She took two cans from the fridge and grabbed some silverware and napkins. By the time she got back to the couch, he had the food spread out on the table, chopsticks waiting. It was all very comfy and cozy. And so different from what she'd had with her previous boyfriends. Wait until she told Jess about this.

They sat on the floor and ate out of the cartons, sharing food and chopsticks. She couldn't quite figure Free out. He'd been pretty hot in the elevator and at the door, but now that they were alone and sitting on the floor eating Chinese food, he didn't flirt or attempt to touch her in any way. He treated her like she was nothing more than a friend. He told her hilarious stories that had her crying with laughter.

Looked like it would be up to her to move things along. She scooted closer to him until her leg brushed his. "So. How do you feel about sleepovers?"

His eyes widened and he choked on his noodles. He continued choking, and Sam took the carton from him and set it on the table. His eyes started to water and he raised his hands high.

"Are you okay?"

He nodded, but coughed some more. He reached for his can of pop and took a gulp. He inhaled slowly, coughing a little more. He slapped his chest and laughed.

"Sorry about that," Sam said with a smile. "I kind of thought that's where we were headed."

"No. I mean, don't worry about it. And yeah, I was hoping we were headed there, too. You just took me by surprise."

She pressed closer, her boobs pushing against his arm, and ran her fingers through his damp hair. "Does that mean you prefer to take the lead with a girl?"

"No. I'm totally comfortable with you in charge. I wasn't expecting it."

"Good," she whispered and licked the shell of his ear.

A shaky breath eased from his mouth.

Sam twisted and straddled him, squeezing between him and the table. It was a tight fit and she liked the way their bodies notched together. She leaned over and kissed him. The heat between them lay thick with need.

Free surged up, which caused her back to crash into the table. She winced.

"Shit. Sorry." He bent his leg and gave the table a kick, but it didn't budge. He released his grip on her and shoved the edge. It barely moved. "So much for my manly strength."

She laughed and kissed him again. "It's the carpet. The legs dig in and it's tough to move."

"You don't have to stroke my ego."

"I can think of better things to stroke."

He groaned and pulled her hips closer. His hard-on pressed against her. Her clit throbbed in response.

"Let's go to my bedroom."

"Wait." His fingers tightened on her hips. "I don't have a condom. I'm not one of those guys who walks around expecting to get laid."

Her smile was so wide, her cheeks stretched. "You knew you were coming to my apartment, right? And you still didn't expect to get laid?"

"I tend to keep my expectations low."

Oh man, did she like this guy. "It's okay. I have some in my room."

"Thank God."

She eased off him and stood. When he joined her, he took her hand and she led him to the bedroom. He stood next to her bed as if he was unsure of his next move. She tugged at the hem of his shirt. Sliding it slowly up, she took note of the slim line of hair on his belly leading into his jeans. It was one of those things that never failed to turn her on. She pulled the shirt over his head.

The movement seemed to spur him into action. He pulled her blouse from her pants and started to unbutton it. His fingers fumbled on the first two. He sighed and closed his eyes.

She covered his hands. "Let me."

Taking her blouse and pants off took no time at all. She reached around to unclasp her bra. Free's hands stilled her. "No."

"What?"

"I just want to look a minute. You're breathtaking."

Her skin warmed everywhere by both the compliment and his hot gaze.

He cupped her jaw and kissed her again, aligning his body with hers. The denim of his jeans rasped against her bare thighs, causing an enticing friction. While he trailed hot, wet kisses down her neck and across her collar, she reached between them and unbuttoned his jeans.

Free nudged her bra strap aside and kissed his way down to her boob. As his mouth greedily latched on to her nipple, she slid her hand into his jeans and allowed her cool fingers to stroke his hot flesh.

He growled with her nipple in his mouth and sucked a little harder. She gasped, but when he tried to pull away, she held his head in place. "More," she added, in case he didn't understand that her gasp was good.

He turned them so he could push her gently

down on the bed. For a moment, they separated. She scooted across the bed to make room for him as he shucked his jeans and underwear. His dick was hard and bobbed as he moved onto the bed.

She spread her thighs. He nestled between them, the thin barrier of her silk panties almost unbearable. He tugged the cup off her still-covered breast and focused his attention on that nipple. Sam's hips wiggled. She needed more.

With Free on top of her, there was little room, but she slid her hand between them and wrapped her fingers around his dick and stroked. He lifted his hips a little to give her more room. He was smooth and hard and hot.

She had just gotten started and he pulled out of her reach. His mouth returned to hers and his hand slid into her panties. He stroked her already-slick folds. She rode his hand and the tension built. "I'm close, Free. Get a condom."

"Where?" His voice was low and scratchy and incredibly sexy.

"Bedside drawer."

He lifted off her and went into the drawer. When she heard the wrapper being opened, she shimmied out of her panties and got rid of her bra.

Free returned and settled between her thighs. She felt the head of his dick prod her opening. Still cautious and hesitant.

She lifted her hips, causing him to enter. As soon as he inched in, he sank deeper with a groan. He started to move and she hooked her calves around his hips. He tilted and swiveled, and like a homing device, he managed to hit the right spot.

Sam threw her head back and dug her nails

into his shoulders. Her heels pressed him closer. He buried his face in her neck. Everything pulsed. She held on to Free as she rode out her orgasm.

As she came down from her high, he stiffened and his muscles flexed. The world felt like it stopped spinning. Time ceased to exist for one glorious moment. They didn't need to breathe or move. They could just be.

It was the one moment during sex that Sam loved the most, more than the stars behind her eyelids and the explosion of nerves. The feeling of weightlessness and freedom.

Then Free crashed against her and she discovered another feeling that she enjoyed: the weight of Free sprawled on top of her. She relished the feel of his body on hers, the soft tickle of his hair on her cheek, the racing of his heart against her chest.

Free propped himself on his elbows and looked directly in her eyes. He said nothing, just stared, and she felt it deep down inside. Then his face broke into a smile, and he dropped a quick kiss on her lips and jumped off the bed. "Be right back."

For a guy who had a hard time with buttons, he moved sure-footedly through her room. She heard water running in the bathroom. Sam rolled to her side and kept her eyes on the door. This was when most guys came back into the room and started picking clothes up off the floor looking for an escape.

She wanted to see what Free's reaction would be. Would he want to spend the night? She tried not to get her hopes up, but she wanted him to stay.

He came back into the room looking less sure of himself than when he'd left. He sat on the edge of the bed. "So about this sleepover…"

"It's not a requirement."

"Is it a real invitation?"

Her heart got tight. "Of course." She patted the bed beside her and he crawled over.

On his way, he grabbed the blanket and covered them. He spooned her with an arm wrapped around her waist.

She relaxed into his embrace and hoped she wasn't making the same mistakes she often did. But then she realized that even though they had spent a lot of time talking over the past few days, this was technically only their second date. Like that was any better than sleeping with a guy on the first date. She had a habit of thinking things were more than they actually were.

"What are you thinking about?"

The question startled her. He'd been so quiet, she'd thought he'd fallen asleep.

"I was just thinking that this is only our second date. And we're in bed together."

He shifted and turned her to face him. "Is that a problem?"

"I don't want you to think that because I have my own condoms that I'm not into monogamy. I am." She blew out a breath that puffed her cheeks. "I'm not seeing anyone else. Are you?"

A low chuckle rumbled in his chest. "I didn't even come here with a condom. What do you think?"

She raised her eyebrow at him.

"No, Samantha. I am not seeing anyone else. I feel like we have a good thing going here."

"We do." She rolled back over. "And Free?"

"Huh?"

"Maybe you should start carrying condoms."

CHAPTER SIX

Samantha stretched out next to Free. Her naked body rubbed against him and her hair tickled his nose. But his morning hard-on demanded more than a cuddle. He rolled over and on top of her, bracing himself on his elbows.

She peeked at him from under heavy eyelids. Then she slapped a hand over her face. "God, don't look at me like that. I'm a mess in the morning."

"You look fine." To prove his point, he prodded her with his dick.

She giggled underneath her hand.

He kissed her neck and down to her tits. "Taste good, too."

"Shut up."

He worked his way down her body, kissing and licking. Her skin was warm and soft. He moved lower, crawling under the blanket covering her. Her body suddenly shifted as she sat up. "What are you doing?"

"Exploring."

"No. Wait."

He flipped the covers off his head and looked up at her. "You don't like oral?"

"It's not that, but—"

He shoved her shoulder. "Just lie back."

She did and her hands covered her face again. Samantha was self-conscious about this? They'd spent the night naked in each other's arms. Hell, she'd stripped in front of him and she seemed fearless.

He nudged her thighs wider with his shoulders and let his fingers play with the juncture where her leg met her pelvis. He smelled her arousal. He lowered his mouth and kissed her. Her muscles were still tense.

Laying a palm flat on her belly, he swiped his tongue across her slit, tasting her fully. His fingers stretched up until he had a handful of tit and tugged on her nipple. Her thighs relaxed a fraction, opening wider, inviting him in.

She tasted like heaven. He swirled the tip of his tongue over her clit and her hips jumped. It was like a damn furnace under the blanket now and he threw it off. She gasped as the cold air hit them, but he sucked on her clit, eliminating any complaint.

His gaze traveled over her body. Her hands no longer covered her face. Her eyes were closed, but she was lost in pleasure. Her fingers tangled in the sheet as she rose up to meet his mouth. He slid a couple of fingers into her and stroked.

She began moaning and her thighs tightened around him.

A bell sounded and he paused.

"Don't you stop."

If nothing else, he was good at taking direction. He flicked his tongue over her and drove his fingers into her until her legs climbed him and she clawed at his head. She released a high-pitched squeal and flopped down. He lapped at her, tasting her come.

He crawled back up her body and reached for a condom. He slid it on while enjoying the post-orgasmic glow on Samantha's face.

A door slammed in the apartment. "Samantha?" a man's voice called.

Free froze. Samantha's eyes bugged out. "Oh my God." She slapped his arm. "Get up. That's my dad."

"Your dad has a key to your apartment?"

She nodded as she jumped off the bed. "He pays for it." Looking at the closed bedroom door, she yelled, "Coming."

Free laughed. "Yeah, you were."

She smacked his shoulder. "Not funny." But she was smiling. "I didn't know he would show up. He never visits." She gave Free a quick kiss on the cheek. "Don't move. Don't leave this room."

He leaned back on the pillows. "Am I a secret?"

"No. But my dad has never liked any of my boyfriends. Ever. I don't want this ruined." She wrapped a robe around her and slipped out the door.

Curiosity got the better of him. He removed the condom and followed to listen at the door.

"Still in bed?" her dad asked.

"I have a guest."

That was it. No explanation. No offer to introduce him.

"We need to talk."

"So you just show up at my apartment?"

"You didn't return my calls."

"I don't want to talk about the car, Dad. My mind's made up."

Free heard some rustling. What if her dad came in here? He looked down. Although his hard-on had subsided, he was still buck naked. Not the way to meet anyone's dad. He grabbed his jeans and hopped into them.

"My boyfriend's an actor."

Seemed weird for Samantha to blurt that out. Then Free remembered he'd left his blaster sitting beside the couch. But she'd called him her boyfriend. It made him smile.

"Emphasis on boy."

That stung.

"I'll be waiting in the car. Say good-bye to the *boy* and meet me in fifteen minutes."

Free sat on the edge of the bed and waited. A minute later, Samantha opened the door.

"Sorry about that. He wants me to have breakfast with him so we can talk." Without even looking at him, she added, "I'm sorry our morning was interrupted."

Her movements were stiff as she moved around the room to gather clothes.

He stood and reached for her arm. "You okay?"

She nodded.

"Want to tell me about it?"

"My dad wants to run my life." She inhaled deeply. "You know how men like him are. I imagine your dad is similar."

Free thought about it, but didn't answer. His dad didn't try to run his life. "Can I help?"

"No. I need to handle this myself." She turned from her dresser with an armful of clothes. "You can take your time and leave whenever you're ready. The door will lock when you close it."

She sighed and her shoulders sank. He hated the defeated nature of her stance. Didn't her father see what he did to her?

"What does he want from you?"

"I'm not even sure. Today it's about the car. He bought it and I gave it back to him."

Free didn't have a response to that. He knew the wrong words would make this conversation take an ugly turn.

"I know it sounds stupid. Trust me. He does it to exert control." She stepped forward and laid her forehead on his shoulder. "I wish I could roll back the clock and be in bed with you."

"Of course you do. I gave you a screaming orgasm and you gave me blue balls."

His comment had the desired effect. She laughed. He wrapped his arms around her and kissed the top of her head. "Be strong. Tell your dad what's important to you."

She leaned back and looked into his eyes. "That's not a quote, is it?"

"No, but this is. *We are who we choose to be. Spider-Man.*"

He kissed her until her body relaxed and her skin was flushed.

"You taste like sex," she whispered against his lips.

"I taste like you." He licked his lips. "You'd

better go. Your dad's waiting and if you keep looking at me like that, he might come back here."

"Call me later."

"I will."

While she was in the shower, he gathered the rest of his clothes and straightened up the bed. Samantha was dressed and ready faster than any other woman he'd ever seen.

She called out a good-bye from the door. He dashed over to catch her before she left.

"Hey. I know you're in a hurry, but I wanted to ask you about New Year's Eve."

Her forehead wrinkled in confusion. "What about it?"

"If you don't have plans, I want to spend it with you. My friends and I throw a party every year. Will you go with me?"

Her whole face brightened with her smile. "Of course." She tilted her head up and kissed him. Then she ran out.

He had hours until he needed to be back at the theater for opening night. In Samantha's kitchen, he found her coffee and made a pot and then took a shower. While he drank a cup of coffee, he cleaned up their dinner mess from the previous night. They'd been too busy to think about the remainder of food. He tossed everything and looked around.

He didn't want to leave, but he shouldn't stay. He wanted to be here when Sam got home, but she'd told him to leave. She might not want him here when she returned. They would definitely talk more about her family. She talked about school and work, but rarely her parents. Now he wondered what the deal was.

He packed his bag and carried his holster with blaster. When he got to the door, he decided he didn't want to just leave, so he dug through a couple of drawers until he found pen and a piece of paper.

I had the best time. We have opening night tonight. Although you've seen it, I'm going to leave you a couple of tickets at Will Call. Bring a friend. The cast goes out after the play. Maybe you can join us. Hope to see you later.

—Free

For the first time in months, he felt good. He liked having a woman in his life, and Samantha eased in as if she belonged there.

As he left her apartment, he sent Hunter a text. **I have a date for the party. Call off the hordes.**

SAM SAT IN THE RESTAURANT AND SIPPED HER lemon water, waiting for her dad to lay in to her.

"You should've returned my calls."

"It was one call. I've been busy with work for the end of the semester."

"That's never prevented you from calling me before. Maybe it's this *boy* you're seeing." He shook out his napkin and laid it across his lap.

"Please don't say it like that. Free is a good guy. He's an actor, but he's in college, graduating this spring."

Her dad *hmph*ed at that.

"Free had nothing to do with me not calling

you back. I didn't call because I didn't want you to try to bully me into taking the car back. I don't want it."

"That's ridiculous. Why wouldn't you want a car?" He drank his water and waved the waiter over.

"Yes, sir."

"Coffee, please." He looked at Sam.

"Me, too."

The waiter left and Sam folded her hands in her lap. "I don't need the car, Dad. Living in the city means I have access to pretty reliable public transportation. I won't have to worry about paying for parking."

"There's something else."

"That car makes me feel like a snob."

"It's a good car."

"I know. Try to put yourself in my shoes. I'm working in neighborhoods that make that car a target. I help people who don't know where their next meal is coming from. And then I drive off in a Mercedes. I feel like a phony and some of the people look at me like that." Her mouth and throat dried as she spoke and she took a cooling drink of water.

"You shouldn't care what they think of you. You're helping them. That's all that should matter."

"I can help them and take the train."

"I worry about you. You're too trusting and naïve."

"I'm not as dumb as you think I am."

The waiter returned with coffee. Her dad waited until the man left before speaking again.

"I've never thought of you as stupid. You are

too trusting. How many times has someone you're helping stolen from you?"

Damn. It was like he had her followed. She couldn't answer him or she'd lose the argument altogether. "I appreciate that you worry about me, but I'm okay. I take the train or bus, and if I'm in an unsafe neighborhood late or I feel uncomfortable, I call a cab."

He said nothing.

She wrapped her hands around her coffee cup. "I need to start living my life and taking care of myself."

He shook his head. "I'm not going to convince you, am I?"

"Nope." Holy crap. Had she just won an argument with her dad? She felt like whooping and hollering through the restaurant. Not only had she won, but he'd actually listened to her. He might not agree with what she said, but he'd listened. "Thank you, Dad."

"For what?"

"For trying to understand where I'm coming from."

"The car will be in the garage if you change your mind."

"I won't. You should sell it." She glanced at her watch. "I have to get going. I have a paper I need to finish this weekend." She stood and left her napkin beside her cup.

He joined her. "Are you going to school or back to your apartment?"

"My apartment."

"I'll drop you off. I'm glad you haven't tried to

give up the apartment." He tossed bills on the table.

She looped her arm around his. "I will, Dad. I just can't swing it until I'm working full-time. I'm not going to live off of you forever. Don't you want me to grow up?"

"Not particularly." He kissed her head and she leaned into him.

When she got back to her apartment, part of her hoped Free would still be there, but as soon as she opened the door, she knew he wasn't. It was a silly hope. He might've had class or work. He couldn't sit around waiting for her all day.

Inside, there was a note stuck to the wall near her coat hook. She couldn't help but smile. Free was a good guy. She held the note as she walked through the apartment. He'd left no overt sign that he'd been there, but he'd cleaned up the mess they'd left.

She would definitely go to the play tonight. Maybe Jess would be free to join her. Then she could see that he wasn't a freak. But first she texted Free.

I'd love to see the play again. Not sure about going out after. I have a paper to finish this weekend. But maybe for a little while.

I'll take whatever I can get. See you later.

As she thumbed through her contacts to call Jess, another text from Free came across.

How did things go with your dad?

Better than expected. I'll tell you about it tonight.

Not just a good guy, but considerate, too. It wouldn't take much for her to completely fall for him. The thought was crazy; she'd only known him for a couple of weeks.

She called Jess to make plans for tonight and to get a dose of sanity.

"Hey, babe. What's up?"

"You want to go out tonight?"

"Sure. Where do you want to go?"

"I have a couple of tickets to see *A Christmas Carol*."

A long pause followed.

"Why?"

"It's opening night and Free is leaving tickets for us."

"This is your latest weirdo?"

"He's not weird and I really like him. Plus, this'll be your chance to meet him and check him out. Then you'll see he's normal."

Jess groaned. "Okay. What time?"

That was one reason she loved Jess. The girl could complain like nobody's business, but she always came through as a friend. They made plans to meet at the theater. If Free passed Jess's test, Sam might think about bringing him to meet her parents. After the holidays, of course. Bringing someone home at Christmas spoke volumes about the relationship and they weren't at that stage. At least not yet.

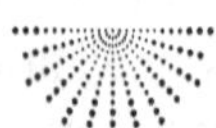

CHAPTER SEVEN

When the curtain came down, Jess stood and stretched. "You were right. It wasn't nearly as bad as I thought it would be."

"Told you." Sam reclined in the theater seat. "I don't know how long it'll take for Free to change, so we might as well stay here."

Jess remained standing and looked across the theater. "Decent-sized crowd."

"I thought they were good. Professional."

Jess plopped back into the seat. "You seem mellow. Why is that? You're usually nervous when I meet a boyfriend for the first time."

"I'm not sure. Free is different. We're comfortable together."

"Seriously?"

"What?"

"You slept with him already."

"I don't know what you're talking about." Sam dodged Jess's stare.

"Spill."

Sam leaned closer to Jess and lowered her voice. "So what? We slept together."

"And?"

"It was sweet and fun. And before you ask, we talked about being exclusive. He's totally on board." She decided to keep his lack of condoms to herself. "He was kind of awkward at first, but he warmed up." She thought about him going down on her moments before her dad barged in. "We were almost caught in the act by my dad."

"Bet that was fun."

"Not." Sam shook her head. "Believe it or not, of all the things my dad could've been upset over, it wasn't Free being in my apartment."

"Seriously?"

"He didn't like that Free's an actor. But even that, he excuses because he assumes I'm playing around. He was more concerned that I won't take back the car."

"Tell him he can send it my way any time."

"You're funny." Her phone buzzed in her pocket and she fished it out. "It's Free. He's says he'll meet us by the front door."

They gathered their things and walked down the aisle. Jess pushed the heavy door to the lobby open and Sam grabbed her arm. "Try to be nice to him."

"I'll be nice as long as he is."

"Then we won't have a problem because I don't think Free knows how to be any other way."

They stood in the lobby for a few minutes before Free found them in the crowd. He got close and then hesitated, like he wasn't sure if he should kiss her. She tilted her lips up in invitation. He pressed a quick kiss and then looked at Jess.

"Hi. I'm Free."

"Jess," she answered, as she looked him up and down.

"Most of the cast is going out for a few drinks if you'd like to join us."

Jess looked at her. Sam slipped her hand into Free's. "I have a paper I need to work on this weekend, but I don't think a little time away would hurt."

"Do you need a ride?"

"No. Jess has her car. We can meet you there."

"I'll text you the address as soon as I get it from someone."

Sam and Jess spent the next couple of hours in a bar with a rowdy crowd of actors and crew members. Sam couldn't remember the last time she'd had so much fun with a group of complete strangers. When she could no longer stifle her yawns, she leaned close to Free and said, "I have to get going. As much as I'd like to stay, I'm really tired and I still have homework."

He held her hand. "You want me to drive you?"

"No. Jess will take me home. Stay with your friends."

He stared at her for a minute. "We're not going to see each other for the rest of the weekend, are we?"

"You're performing and I have schoolwork, so probably not." The thought made her stomach sink.

"How about Tuesday or Wednesday night?"

Crap. "I work on Tuesday and I have plans

Wednesday. Unless you want to come wrap presents for the shelter. We order pizza and have a wrapping party. It usually goes pretty late."

"Tell me when and where and I'll be there."

"Are you serious?"

"Why not? I get to spend the evening with my girlfriend. I don't care what we're doing." He leaned closer and his breath tickled her ear. "I'll only care what we do after the wrapping is done."

His suggestion sent tingles through her body. Was there really no way to have a date before then? Coffee together wasn't enough anymore. She closed her eyes. *Be an adult, Sam. Get your work done.* "Call me tomorrow."

When she stood with Jess, he joined them.

"I'll walk you out."

Jess waved at them. "How about I go get the car and bring it to the door so I don't have to witness anymore lovebird crap."

Free laughed. "It was nice to meet you, Jess."

"You, too." She walked through the crowd and out the door.

Free held her coat out for her to put on and told his friends he'd be right back. At the front door to the bar, he slid his arm around her back. "I'm glad you came out tonight."

"So am I. I liked meeting your friends."

"Did I pass the test?"

Sam smiled. "You mean Jess? She's not a test." Well, maybe a little. "I think you did okay."

"What would happen if I didn't?"

"I'd have to dump you and burn your number, of course."

"Very funny." He leaned in and kissed her. His

lips were soft, and he tasted like the beer he'd drunk.

She sighed into him, wishing for more. A horn honked outside.

Free pulled away. "That's your ride."

"Coffee Monday?"

"Absolutely."

He stood at the door and watched until she was safely in Jess's car. She smiled and waved as Jess pulled away.

"How long have you known this guy?"

Sam shrugged. "A few weeks I guess."

"You have it so bad."

"What?"

"And he's no better. The two of you sitting at the table tonight… I don't even have the words. It was like you were part of the group, but all you cared about was each other."

Sam squinted at her friend and replayed the night at the bar. "Free talked to his friends all night."

"But he was touching you, checking on you, making sure you were good in between each sentence of conversation."

Sam couldn't argue. "Given that my past boyfriends had a habit of forgetting I was around, I kind of like it."

"I'm not saying you shouldn't. It just seems like you're falling really hard really fast."

She was. She felt it every time she looked at Free or talked to him. Was that a bad thing? Keeping her thoughts to herself, she looked out the window and watched the city fly by.

Jess had her best interests in mind. Sam knew

she fell fast for guys, but this felt different, mutual in ways it hadn't in the past. She didn't need any seeds of doubt planted in her new relationship.

She resolved to let it go at its own pace.

FREE'S WEEKEND HAD GONE AS WELL AS HE'D expected. Opening weekend was always exhausting and exhilarating. The only thing that would've been an improvement would've been if he'd had more time with Samantha. But he'd get to see her for a bit this afternoon after Cary's workout. Maybe they could go to dinner since he didn't have to worry about rehearsal.

His classes were almost over, with only one final to take this week. He walked into his dad's downtown office. He loved coming here, especially knowing that in a few short months he would have a permanent spot. He waved at his dad's secretary, who was on the phone. She nodded and waved him to the office door.

Free knocked once to announce himself and then eased the door open in case his dad was on the phone, as well.

"Free, glad you could stop by."

"It felt a little more like you were expecting me, not inviting me."

"You're funny." He pointed to the seat in front of the desk. "You were dead-on with the reports I gave you. Can't wait to get you on board."

Free unbuttoned his coat and his dad looked at the costume he wore. He'd left the Zorro mask and hat in the car, but the all-black outfit was still telling. "Going to work out with Cary?"

Free nodded. "What did I need to come here for?"

"I know you're busy with the play until Christmas, which your mother loved by the way. She can't stop singing your praises to everyone." He leaned his elbows on his desk. "I want you to come to the office holiday party this year."

Free opened his mouth to refuse, but his dad stopped him with a hand in the air. "The party is on the twenty-ninth, so it won't interfere with the play or the party you throw with the guys. You need to start networking with our clients."

Free hated the thought of networking. He excelled with numbers and money. Having to sell himself to people was not a strong suit. It was part of why he wanted to work for his dad instead of finding another firm. No interview required.

"I don't work here yet. I don't see what good will come of it."

"I want people to see your face, meet our newest associate who will be joining us this summer. Your hands have been on many of these projects. I want our clients to become comfortable with you." He leaned back in his chair and waited for Free to come up with his next rebuttal.

The problem was, Free didn't have one. His father believed in a hands-on approach with his clients and he expected it of his employees. Clients were not simply account numbers. Free knew this and he respected it.

"You know this isn't a good idea, Dad. I know the clients. You've taught me well, but I suck at the stupid small talk. I don't know how to shoot the breeze with someone. If they want to discuss their portfolios, I can oblige, but I don't want to talk about whether I think we'll get more snow or if the Bears have a shot this year."

His dad laughed. "We're sure to get more snow. It is Chicago, after all, and the Bears are out of it again."

Free shook his head. "You know what I mean."

"You'll be fine. I expect you to be here just like every other employee. Your brother never has a problem coming to the party."

"That's because Cary is a people person. He loves being surrounded by a bunch of people where he can tell funny stories. I tell a story and all I get are looks, not laughs." Unlike at the gym, where Free knew he'd get the laughs. Cary didn't mind being the center of attention at a party where the focus was on his words, unlike at the gym where everything was about his body. Cary could single-handedly carry a party.

"Time to grow up, Humphrey. This is part of the job, like it or not. As long as you don't do anything to embarrass us, you'll be fine."

Free stood to leave. Everything his dad wanted was easier said than done. He knew arguing wouldn't do him a bit of good. He needed to just figure out how to get through the night without embarrassing himself or his dad. If he kept his mouth shut, he might succeed.

"You'll need to wear a good suit, no costumes." He pointed at Free. "And maybe not discuss the acting. Our clients want to know their advisers are serious professionals."

"I know." He understood his dad's stance. Although his dad adored his mom and her love of theater, he only tolerated it in Free. He never tried to stop Free from acting, but he didn't exactly support it, either. It was the part of Free they didn't talk about much.

He said good-bye and left the office. Tension tightened his muscles. He had a little over a week to figure out how to network. A week to learn how to network with clients on top of studying for one more final, acting in a play, and trying to spend time with his new girlfriend.

Girlfriend. He liked the sound of that. Maybe he should invite Samantha to the company party. She was a social worker, which by definition made her a people person. She would probably make a good buffer. As he drove to the coffee shop for their usual mini-date, he debated the merits of asking her to the party.

She wouldn't embarrass him. She would know how to talk to people. She had a way of making people around her relax. He'd get to spend another evening with her while accomplishing what he needed to do.

However, bringing her to his father's—and soon to be his—place of business screamed of a serious relationship. While he had no problem with that, he couldn't predict how Samantha would react. Or his father, for that matter. Free wasn't in the habit of bringing too many girls home to meet his parents.

Throughout Cary's entire workout, Free was distracted by his conversation with their dad. Although Cary could sympathize with Free, he never understood Free's inability to function at cocktail parties and things like that. A party filled with his friends, he was fine with. It was the strangers who did him in.

As they walked back to the locker room, Cary asked, "Where's your head today, man? You haven't cracked one joke."

"Other stuff on my mind."

"Like the reason you didn't make it home last week?"

"Yeah, Samantha is part of it. I have a lot going on right now."

"Anything I can help with?"

Free shook his head. "Not now."

"If you're sure. See you at home later?"

"Yeah. Take these for me, will you?" He handed Cary the hat and sword and stuffed the eye mask in his pocket. He left the gym and walked the short distance to the shop. Samantha was already seated at a table instead of waiting in line for him like she usually did. She had two cups of coffee in front of her and her laptop open. Her face brightened when she saw him. He didn't think he'd ever get used to that feeling.

"Hi." He kissed her cheek, which was warm against his cold lips. Since he enjoyed her soft cheek, he moved to take her lips. At the contact, his muscles eased a fraction.

"Hello," she said against his lips when he pulled back. "Cute fake mustache."

"I am Zorro." He took the seat across from her. "You didn't need to buy my coffee for me."

"It's not like you have a complicated order for me to remember. Plus, I wanted to save a few minutes to show you this." She pointed at the laptop.

"What?"

"You know all those pictures I took of you in your costumes?" She bubbled with excitement. "I uploaded them to Reddit." She turned the screen to face him.

He sat, stunned, as she scrolled down the page.

"I think what you're doing for Cary is huge, and I wanted you to be recognized for the good deed. I wanted people to know that there are people who do selfless things. What I didn't expect is this." She pointed at the screen where a list of photos of him in costume stared back. "In the last hour, I've gotten over two hundred comments."

Free flicked his gaze at her and then back at the screen. His heart raced faster than it had on his very first opening night. Thousands of people would see this. His stomach knotted. "You shouldn't have done this."

"Why? It's no big deal. Read the comments. Sure, there are some that are trolls who say horrible things about you, but most of them are written by people who are truly impressed with you. You should be proud of yourself."

"I didn't do this for recognition. And crap. My dad will hate this." Anger and confusion boiled up in his chest. The frustration over his father's expectations and the surprise hit from Samantha had him clamping his jaw tight. He tried to tell himself that she meant well.

"This is good, Free. People are commenting on how good your costumes are and how well you transform yourself. They can see what a good actor you are."

He closed the laptop. "But I don't want this kind of attention. I'm sure Cary wouldn't appreciate it. The whole idea of me dressing up was to draw attention *away* from him."

She stiffened. "I wasn't trying to embarrass Cary. I thought you'd like the recognition."

"You thought wrong. Please tell me you didn't use my name."

Her face dropped and a rock settled in his gut.

"No. I wasn't trying to invade your privacy. I thought this would be fun. I'm sorry."

He'd upset her, and the look on her face scared him a little, but he couldn't console her right now. He was pissed. She'd taken something that was personal and laid it out for the whole world to see. This wasn't him onstage where he expected an audience. This was about helping his brother.

He thought she understood that.

"I need to go. I'll talk to you later."

He turned and walked out the door without looking back. He didn't even remember to grab his coffee.

The tension and frustration he'd felt after meeting with his dad returned twofold, and he had no idea how to make it disappear.

CHAPTER EIGHT

Free left the coffee shop with no real plan. He was mad and frustrated and didn't know what to do about it. Before long, he found himself pulling into the lot of Comic Universe. Adam's mom owned the place, and although Adam worked there, Free always associated it as their place to hang out. At least it had been through high school. With the demands of college and work, they didn't hang out in the store too much anymore.

He walked into the shop and stood for a moment to let the peace wash over him. The place never changed. Adam's mom, Bonnie, often talked about moving things around or rearranging the entire store, but she never did. He could find any series in the store even if he was blindfolded. Adam stood at his desk, seemingly oblivious to his entrance.

"Hey," Free called.

Adam looked over his shoulder as he put a paper on his drawing desk. Adam had mentioned that he was working on a comic anthology with a girl he'd met at the shop. From the look on Adam's face, the drawing wasn't going well. "What are you doing here?"

"Shitty day, so I thought I'd come hang out."

"No rehearsal?"

"Opening weekend just passed, so we're getting a break."

"What about the new girl? Hunter said you found a date to the party." He leaned against the counter by the register.

Free took off his coat and laid it on the glass. "I did. Her name is Samantha, and right now, I'm kind of pissed at her."

"It's never good if the fighting starts this early in a relationship."

"It's not a fight. She did something and I got mad. I might've overreacted, but I was already frustrated with my dad."

"Where do you want to start? Samantha or your dad?"

"Samantha's been taking pictures of me in costume when we meet for coffee. She snaps a shot on her phone after Cary's workout. I thought nothing of it when she asked. I figured she had a good laugh about it. Then today, she tells me she uploaded the pictures to Reddit with the story explaining why I'm dressing up."

"Oh."

"I don't know what she was thinking."

"It's a pretty damn good story."

Free let out a huge sigh. Yeah, he'd overreacted to Samantha's actions. "I never thought about it being a story. I was worried about my brother."

"But it's the kind of headline people click on from Yahoo or Buzzfeed."

Adam was right. He'd click if it hadn't been about him. "I just came from meeting with my dad, so I was already kind of wound up. He wants me to come to the company holiday party to network. As if that's not bad enough, he felt the need to point out that I should leave the costumes and actor talk at home. When I got to the coffee shop to meet with Sam, I just wanted to relax."

"You were a total dick, weren't you?"

Free stared at his friend.

"I know you. You're like the most laid-back person until you freak out. Going to the party freaked you out and then the idea of your dad seeing the Reddit post pushed you over the edge. I don't even need to know what you said or did. Just call her and apologize."

The upside to having friends who knew you as long as Adam and Hunter had was that they didn't mince words. They'd call your bullshit without even blinking. Of course, Adam was right. He needed to apologize.

Free walked around the counter and sat on a stool near Adam. "I'm dreading the party."

"It's just a stupid cocktail party."

"I know my job. My dad knows I know it. I'm a numbers guy, but he wants me to network. I suck at it."

"I'm no social wonder, but even I can manage a cocktail party. You do fine at our parties."

"Those parties are filled with people I already know. We have things to talk about." He straightened the cuffs on his long sleeves.

"Maybe you're looking at this all wrong. Treat it like any other role you play."

Adam's words were like a light in a closet. Free had no idea why the thought had never occurred to him before. He'd spent so much time keeping those two parts of his life separate that he hadn't considered how he could use the skills from one to help in the other.

He'd have to give some more thought to who he'd need to be. Although the Doctor would be his automatic choice, he wasn't sophisticated enough.

"Have you asked Samantha to be your date for New Year's Eve?"

"Yeah, assuming she'll still come after today. How about you? You have a date?"

"Kind of."

"Cop-out."

"Reese agreed to be my date, but she's not my girlfriend or anything. We're just working together, and when Hunter started talking about the party, I blurted out that she was my date."

Free studied his friend's face. "You blurted something. Now I know you're full of shit. You don't blurt. Maybe the real question is why she isn't your girlfriend."

"Because I don't want her to be."

"Why not?"

"It's complicated." Adam hopped off his stool and walked to the other side of the counter.

"Did you have sex?"

"No, but I made the mistake of kissing her and now I can't stop thinking about it. We're better off as friends, though, especially working together."

"You say that like you're trying to convince me, but I think it's you who needs the convincing."

"Shut up." Adam suddenly became invested in reorganizing a box of comics.

"Hunter's right. We are pitiful. Did you at least buy Reese a Christmas present?"

Adam nodded. "We're not going to see each other on the holiday or anything, but I have something to give to her at the party."

"I don't know what to get for Samantha. We've only been on a couple of dates, but I did spend the night at her apartment. She's my girlfriend, but it's new." Free stood and walked down an aisle brushing his fingers over the comic books. "There should be some kind of guidebook for guys like us."

"Keep it simple. I got Reese a Batgirl bobblehead doll and some notebooks that she likes to write in."

"That doesn't help."

"What does Samantha like?"

"Fancy coffee. Books." Shit, that was lame. He didn't even know what things his new girlfriend liked. Made it hard to plan for a gift.

"Get her coffee and flowers. All girls like flowers." Adam sounded relieved not to be discussing his own sad love life.

They left the topic of women and discussed the New Year's Eve party and comics for a while before Free decided to leave. He had plenty to think about, starting with an apology.

Sam didn't know how things had gone so wrong with Free. He was so upset, he didn't even drink his coffee. She'd deleted the post as soon as he'd left, and she sincerely hoped that no one had copied it anywhere else. After all, it had only been up a couple of hours.

She really wished Free could understand that the attention could be a good thing for him. She'd thought a little exposure might garner him more acting jobs. Any publicity was good, right? At least she'd thought so.

Once home, she kicked off her heels and changed into her faded yoga pants and ripped T-shirt along with fluffy socks. She eyed her computer, knowing she had to finish the case study and submit it before the end of the week. It was the last assignment for the semester, then she was free. To be with Free.

She opened a bottle of wine and thought about calling him to apologize again. He'd had some time to cool off, so they could probably talk. What if she called and he didn't answer? Then her mind would wander about where he might be and she'd start to think he was like her previous boyfriends. But Free was different and she refused to give in to that way of thinking.

With her glass of wine, she opened her laptop and the case study. She'd need the wine to get through it. She loved the idea of being a social worker, but she had yet to learn how to distance herself from the problems of the people she worked with. Her eyes filled with tears as she reread her notes on the young girl who had been removed from her home because of abuse.

This wasn't even a real child that she knew. Her professor had issued samples for the class to write up and defend how they would approach a client. After another sip of wine to fortify her, she dove in and began typing. Paperwork shouldn't upset her. It was the most mundane part of the job.

Fifteen minutes into working, her phone buzzed with a text from Free.

I'm in the area. If you're home, I'd like to come over.

Her stomach flipped. Surely, if he were still upset, he wouldn't want to see her. She stared at the computer screen. If Free came over, there was the distinct possibility that this paper wouldn't get finished tonight. So she'd work until he arrived. **I'm home.**

He didn't say how close he was or how long it would take, so she called down to the doorman and told him to send Free up when he arrived. In the meantime, she focused on her case study. By the time she finished writing the narrative for the child, tears streamed down her face.

And then there was a knock on her door. Shit. She hadn't thought Free would get there so quickly. She swiped at the tears and took a quick gulp of wine.

Sam opened the door with a smile, but Free's face was filled with something other than happiness at seeing her. Maybe he was still pissed.

"What's wrong?" He rushed through the door and cradled her face with both of his hands. His thumbs caressed her cheeks.

"Nothing."

"You've been crying."

She rolled her eyes. "I was working on my final case study for the semester and the story of this kid makes me sad."

Instead of stepping away from her and laughing, he leaned forward and kissed her lips gently. He eased back and rested his forehead against hers. "I'm sorry," he whispered.

"It's the job. I need to get a thicker skin so it doesn't get to me so easily."

"I'm sorry for everything, especially the way I acted at the coffee shop."

"I'm sorry, too. I had no malicious intent."

Now he did laugh. "I never considered that. I don't think it's even possible."

As he pulled away, his fingers brushed her skin so achingly gently that she wanted to curl around him and beg for more. He held her hand and led her to the couch. They sat and Free stared at their linked hands.

"I love to dress up and act. It's part of who I am. I know that when I get up on a stage, people are going to stare at me. When I started dressing up so Cary would work out, my entire intention was to get people to stare at me so he'd be more comfortable. But it was always about him."

Sam nodded. "I know. I just wanted other people to know that people like you are out there doing selfless things."

"What if the story gets bigger, gains traction? People would be all over Cary. And like I said, my dad would hate it."

"I already deleted it. The post is gone, so I doubt it'll gain traction anywhere. As soon as you left, I deleted it." She stood and walked to get her glass of wine. She took a gulp without turning around. "I spend so much time surrounded by horrific things. People who have had cruel things done to them. You are a bright spot in my day. I just wanted others to see."

Suddenly his arms were back around her. "Why do you do it?"

"Because they need help. I feel like I'm making a difference."

"I'm glad I can be a bright spot for you. You're much more than that for me, and I feel like a total shit for the way I acted. I had a frustrating day and I took it out on you."

She set her glass down and turned in his arms. "Next time, just say so."

"I'll try. In case you haven't noticed, words aren't always my friends."

"I think you do fine." She ran her hands down his chest and torso. Then lower. "I know an excellent way to ease frustration."

"You do?" He swallowed hard while she stroked him through his pants.

She nodded. "Go have a seat on the couch. You want a glass of wine?"

"Sure." He backed away from her, his eyes not leaving hers until she turned to the kitchen to get a glass. She poured the wine and took it to him. After he accepted the glass, she knelt in front of him. Leaning forward, she started to unbutton his shirt, kissing the exposed skin.

When she reached for the button on his pants, he jumped and grabbed his glass with two hands. "What are you doing?"

"Easing your frustration by returning the favor from the other morning." With a gentle hand on his chest, she pushed him back. "Enjoy your wine, but don't spill it. I like this couch."

She undid the pants and nudged him to lift his hips so she could pull them down. His skin was hot to the touch and his dick was already hard. With her fist, she stroked him a couple of times before leaning forward and wrapping her lips around the head. She swirled her tongue over the tip and Free groaned.

He was going to make this easy if he was groaning already. Instead of dropping her whole mouth over him, she licked his shaft on the underside to the base and then back up. His left hand gripped the edge of the couch as he watched her. He took a swig of wine, then reached to put the glass down. She took it from him and set it on the table behind her.

She stroked him with her hand again as she lowered her mouth to lick his balls. His hips jumped at the contact. She trailed her tongue up his length and then took him into her mouth. On her way up, she hollowed her cheeks for maximum contact. When the head slipped from her lips with a *pop*, he shifted again, raising his hips, silently asking for more.

Sam obliged. This time, she went down on him and began to bob. Her lips met her fist at the base, pumping a rhythm. Free's head fell back against the couch and he closed his eyes. His hands stilled at his sides, palms down, fingers spread wide, pressing into the cushion.

He held pretty tight to his control. More than most guys she'd been with. "Touch me, Free."

His eyes opened and he picked up his hands, but he didn't move to touch her. She grabbed his hand and placed his palm on her head, giving him the permission he must've needed. She went back to sucking him and loved the way his fingers tightened the grip on her hair. His other hand came to her shoulder, massaging and squeezing.

His hips rose to meet her mouth and Sam knew he was close. She moved faster, sucking and licking.

"Sam." Free tried to push up to stop her.

She slapped her palm on his chest and continued. Her nails rasped over his skin as he spurted into her mouth. She swallowed until he stopped moving. His hand slid off her head.

Sam rocked back on her haunches. "Hope that makes up for the blue balls."

"Christ, that was good."

She smirked and drained his wineglass. "More?"

"Not wine. Give me a few minutes and I'll take care of you."

"This wasn't a quid-pro-quo situation. I gave you a blow job because I wanted to." She stood with the empty glass. "And you can't spend the night. I have to finish this paper."

"I can wait for you to finish."

As tempting as that was, she shook her head. "If you're here, I won't get my work done."

He tucked himself back into his pants. "Are we still on for tomorrow night?"

"You still want to wrap presents with me?"

"Of course." He wrapped a hand on her hip. "I get to spend the night tomorrow, though, right?"

"As long as I finish this case study tonight."

He smacked her ass. "Then get to work. I'll see you tomorrow."

After pulling his coat on, he came back for another kiss. "Don't cry. Just do the job."

She kissed him back and wished she knew how to do that, to separate parts of herself. One more thing to work on before graduation.

CHAPTER NINE

By the time Christmas came, Sam was floating. She and Free had spent most of the week together prior to the holiday. Not only had he shown up to help wrap presents for the shelter, but he then volunteered to dress as Santa to distribute the gifts. Both the mothers and the kids loved meeting Santa. Seeing Free in that role was probably her favorite. It was the epitome of who he was: a caring guy who wanted to make people smile.

They'd spent the night together on Christmas Eve eve and exchanged gifts. She bought Free a TARDIS cookie jar and filled it with homemade cookies. He had dressed as the Riddler and sent her on a treasure hunt through her apartment for her gift—a Batgirl costume. Then he proceeded to kidnap Batgirl and have his way with her. They lay in bed and shared the cookies she baked.

It was the best holiday ever.

She'd decided that although she and Free wouldn't be together for Christmas Day, she was going to tell her parents about him. She wanted them to know how serious their relationship was. In fact, she wanted them to meet him as soon as possible.

Christmas morning, Free had texted her to tell her to have fun with her family. At her house, Christmas was an all-day affair. They had breakfast with just the immediate family and they opened gifts. Then in the late afternoon, extended family arrived for a huge meal and more gifts and catching up. She was glad that she and Free had decided not to try to push togetherness over the holiday. She had a feeling he'd be overwhelmed. This way, he had a whole year to get used to her family in smaller doses.

She had no doubt they'd still be together in a year. They fell in sync so quickly, she couldn't imagine it being any other way.

As she finished her breakfast, she looked at her parents. "Mom, Dad, I have something to tell you."

"You want the car back," her dad announced.

"No, sorry to disappoint you." She took a deep breath. "I'm involved with someone and it's pretty serious."

Her dad placed his fork against his plate with a slight *clink*. "Not the actor."

Sam barely refrained from rolling her eyes. "Yes, Dad, the actor. He's not like any other guy I've ever dated."

"That's a good thing."

Man, Dad's on a roll today.

"I'm falling for him, and I want you to meet him after the holidays."

Vanessa stood and kissed Sam's cheek. "I'm happy for you, baby."

"How long have you been seeing this boy?"

She hated the way her father insisted on calling Free a "boy." "About a month."

"Then it's not all that serious."

"It is."

"Michael, don't ruin the holiday."

"I'm not ruining anything, Vanessa. Samantha explained that she wants to be independent. I simply can't be on board with that when she routinely shows poor judgment."

Sam pushed away from the table. "I do not show poor judgment. I'm sorry you still don't approve of who I date."

She carried her empty plate to the kitchen. She wasn't sure what she'd expected from her dad. In a way, she'd done this to herself by dating every guy she could who would make him crazy. After drinking a glass of water, she decided that she'd have to make her dad see that Free was different.

She returned to her seat in the dining room. "I'm sorry for walking out." She rubbed her hands down her smooth skirt. "I realize that I've dated quite a few men that you didn't approve of."

"With good reason."

Sam smiled. "Probably. But Free is different. He's sweet and kind."

"But he's an actor. How is he going to support himself?"

The question sank into Sam. Her dad was afraid Free was another guy who wanted to use her for her money. "The same way the rest of us do."

Her dad continued to look at her as if waiting for further explanation.

"Before you ask, he hasn't ever asked me for a dime. He's paid when we go out, so that's already an improvement over like seventy-five percent of my past boyfriends." She laughed and felt a bit relieved when her dad cracked a smile.

Vanessa stood. "I think it's time for presents." She rushed out of the room toward the living room and the Christmas tree.

Sam stood. "Are we okay?"

Michael put his arm around her shoulder. "I'd like you to attend a holiday party with me for business."

Sam groaned. She'd gone to a few business parties with her dad over the years and they all had one thing in common: They were boring.

"I want you to meet a different class of men."

"I just told you that I'm in a serious relationship."

"That's only a month old."

"You should still respect it." Sam sat on the couch as her dad took his favorite armchair. It had been in that chair that he'd read *The Little Engine That Could* to her as a child.

"I have a hard time respecting a man who won't be able to support his family, one who doesn't have a real job."

Sam leaned forward and accepted the gift her mom handed her. "Just because he doesn't work from nine to five doesn't mean it's not a real job. And he doesn't have a family to support."

"But if it's as serious as you'd have me believe, he would be thinking in those terms." He pointed to the present in her lap, urging her to open it.

As she peeled the paper away from the box, her

dad continued, "I'm not asking you to break up with him. I've learned my lesson with that. I'm only asking you to attend a party with me and keep an open mind."

With paper tossed to the side, Sam held the box on her lap. "If I go to this party and no one piques my interest, you'll leave me alone and be nice to Free when you meet him?"

"I can try if you can."

Sam slid a finger along the edge of the box to break the tape she knew her mother would have placed there. "Deal." She had no worries. Sam couldn't imagine any guy at her dad's business gathering would draw her eye. Even if they were good-looking, they always ended up sounding too much like her dad, where money was the be-all and end-all to life.

She wanted more.

IT HAD BEEN DAYS SINCE FREE HAD SEEN SAM. HE'D wanted to invite her to his dad's company party, but she'd already said that she was busy with her parents that night. By the time the party rolled around, Free had managed to work himself into a frenzy of freakishness. He sat on his bed staring into his closet of costumes. He knew he couldn't don one tonight, but he needed the inspiration to get through the evening.

He glanced at the new suit his dad insisted on buying him. Cary leaned against the door frame. "It won't bite. I promise."

"I know."

"Don't be nervous. It's just a party. These people are already clients. You don't need to convince them of anything."

"That makes it worse. I could sell my skills. I excel at talking numbers. I'm not good at selling myself."

Cary crossed his arms. "You managed to sell yourself to a beautiful girl."

"I'm still trying to figure that one out." He flopped back on the bed. "I was in character when I won her over. I didn't have to be me."

The mattress dipped as Cary sat on the corner. "Even in costume, you're still you. And if you didn't show her yourself, she wouldn't still be going out with you."

"Adam told me to treat tonight like I'm playing a role. I can't figure out who to be."

Cary smacked his thigh. "That's easy. If you're not going to be yourself, be Bond."

"I thought it was Be Batman."

Cary laughed. "You'll never have the muscles for Batman, but you can pull off Bond."

This time, Free laughed. James Bond was a suave womanizer. Even on his best day, Free failed at simple flirting. He had, however, seen all of the James Bond films.

Free rolled off the bed and stood in front of the new suit. It was a badass suit.

"Get dressed and we'll go together. I'll show you the ropes." Cary stood and left the room. Too bad Cary didn't have that confidence at the gym. Cary had been a shy kid but he'd learned early that people liked to laugh. So he had an anecdote for every situation.

If Free could learn that one skill, he'd survive socializing, but Free knew he tended to just sound like a nerd, so he kept his mouth shut.

He dressed in the suit and felt oddly comfortable in it. Although he'd worn suits when interning with his dad over the summers, he rarely ever wore them during the school year. Slipping into one now made him feel like he was headed into the office. Being in the office relaxed him. There he only had to worry about numbers. Numbers made sense. People didn't.

Sam was proof of that. Not only did he have a hard time wrapping his head around her actually liking him, but the things she saw while volunteering cemented how little people made sense. Yet she forged ahead day after day in an attempt to make a difference. He respected her for it, but he couldn't fully understand. He knew he couldn't do that.

When he left his room, Free stopped in the hall at the sight of Cary. He saw his brother dressed in a suit most days, but he, too, had a new suit courtesy of their father. He looked amazing. The weight loss was noticeable. Without a doubt, Cary would steal the show tonight.

They drove to the banquet hall together, Cary filling the silence with information about clients. Cary knew names of family members and hobbies and general happenings in the lives of their clients. It was one of the reasons people gravitated toward him. Free listened intently, making mental notes. If Cary pointed these people out at the party, he might actually be able to make conversation.

Maybe he should just stick to Cary's side and

let him lead. Free could jump in with an occasional question so people knew he was paying attention, but he wouldn't have to initiate anything. Another plan hatched. It would be the gym scenario in reverse.

By the time they parked, Free was feeling more confident about the party. Inside, they were directed to one of the small banquet rooms. Their parents were there already, as were a few others. Free recognized some of the employees, so he figured no clients had arrived yet.

"Boys, glad you came early." Anthony Mitchell spoke with his arms wide in welcome for his sons. With some men, the gesture might seem fake, but with Anthony, it was genuine. Their dad was happy to have them as part of his firm.

"Hi, Dad."

Cary didn't speak, but turned and reached for a couple of glasses of champagne from a passing waiter. He handed one to Free. "Sip slowly, but keep it in your hand as a prop. You'll fidget less."

"Cary, that suit looks good. It shows off that sexy body." Amelia kissed Cary's cheek. Cary was much like her in that they both excelled at working a crowd. Here, they were in their element.

Free took a sip of champagne and wished it was a beer. He closed his eyes and imagined Bond —always calm, ready for a fight or sex, impeccable. Visualization worked when preparing for a role, and he depended on it to work now. When he reopened his eyes, his mother stood in front of him.

"Let's walk." She looped her arm through his

and led him away from Cary and Anthony. "You have nothing to be nervous about. You're already guaranteed a job after graduation. Thank God for nepotism."

"I'd like to think Dad's hiring me because I'm capable."

"Of course he is. So, who are you tonight?"

"Bond, James Bond."

"Perfect selection. Come with me to speak to the caterer about the hors d'oeuvres. I'm afraid they'll rush them out before too many people arrive. I want them staggered."

Free led her to the kitchen, grateful for the reprieve. As she spoke to the manager, Free saw clients arriving and checking their coats. The curtain was up and there was no turning back.

After going to the open bar to exchange his champagne for a beer, Free sought out Cary. He found him quickly, already entertaining a client. Free sidled up to the group and waited to be introduced.

When there was a break in the conversation, Cary said, "I'd like you to meet my brother, Humphrey. He interned this past summer, and he'll be joining us full-time after graduation."

Free extended his hand.

The man took it. "James Wheeler." He pointed to Cary. "We were just discussing baseball. Tell me, Humphrey, are you a Sox fan or a Cubs fan?"

"Uh, neither. I don't really follow sports."

"What do you follow?"

"The stock market."

For whatever reason, the man found Free's honesty funny and barked out a laugh. Although he wasn't trying to be entertaining, Free would take laughter over the usual blank stare he got from some people. He sipped his beer and waited for the laughter to subside. "So what business are you in, Mr. Wheeler?"

"I've got my fingers in a few pies, but tonight's not about discussing business." He looked at Free's glass. "Is that beer?"

Free nodded, sure he'd managed to screw up by indulging in the wrong kind of drink.

Mr. Wheeler put his champagne glass on the table. "Point me in the direction to get a beer."

"I'll walk you over. It's an open bar." Cary nodded at Free to encourage him. Maybe tonight wouldn't be as bad as Free had thought.

CHAPTER TEN

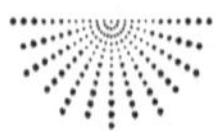

As Sam stepped out of her father's car, she smoothed a hand down her little black dress. She'd dressed to impress her dad and to take the evening seriously. She'd speak to the stuffy suits that her dad thought were better for her than Free, but she knew in her heart, none of them had a chance.

She joined her parents and they walked through the doors of the banquet hall as a family. Sam wondered how many other businessmen brought their families. Her dad said that the banking firm was family-run and family-oriented and they welcomed everyone at the annual party. She couldn't remember ever attending before, so she might've refused the invitation.

Inside, they checked their coats and within moments, waiters passed by with trays of champagne and hors d'oeuvres. Sam grabbed a glass and a crab cake. She surveyed the room. A sea of dark suits filled the space. She sighed, thinking of Free and his many costumes.

Trailing behind her parents, Sam munched on

the crab cake and waited to see exactly what her dad had planned. Did he hope to simply introduce her to a bunch of random single guys in suits and pray for a love connection?

Her dad stopped to talk to someone and she took the moment to snag another crab cake. As she popped it in her mouth, her dad turned and said, "This is my daughter, Samantha. Samantha, this is Anthony Mitchell. Samantha is studying to be a social worker. No matter how hard I tried, I couldn't sell her on the idea of following in my footsteps."

Sam chewed as quickly as possible and brushed her fingers on her napkin before extending her hand. "Nice to meet you," she said as soon as her mouth was empty.

"I'm always happy to meet the next generation of investors," Anthony said.

"Sorry to disappoint you, but I don't think I'll make all that much money as a social worker to have to worry about investments."

He shook a finger at her. "Everyone needs to plan for the future. My son is about your age. He could convince you." He stretched to look over her head and called, "Humphrey, come here."

Sam's heart stuttered. No way could there be another guy her age with that name. She turned and saw Free walking toward her. He looked nothing like her boyfriend. He blended perfectly into the crowd of suits.

His eyes widened and he stumbled over his own feet, but then smiled at her. He reached for her hand. "Hey, what are you doing here?"

She waved a hand at her dad. "I came with my

parents." Her mouth dried as she scanned his appearance again, searching for some sign of Free. Not even red Converse sneakers.

"You two know each other?" her dad asked.

She released Free's hand and turned to her dad. "This is Free, my boyfriend."

Anthony chuckled. "Then I guess your investments are already in excellent hands."

Free's brow wrinkled at his dad's comment. He looked at her parents and said, "Mr. and Mrs. Wolf, it's nice to meet you." He shoved a hand forward in greeting. Her parents shook briefly while Sam stared in awe.

"Let's leave the kids alone," Anthony said, drawing their attention. Her parents followed him to the bar.

Sam's chest became tight with confusion. "What are you doing here?"

"My dad wanted me to be here to network."

"Network for what?" Seeing him now, in this suit, talking about networking and investments, made her stomach sink. She wasn't going to like his answer.

"He wants the clients to be familiar with me before I start work this summer."

"You're going to work for your dad? What about acting?"

He shrugged. "Acting is a hobby. I'll continue to do a few shows a year because I enjoy it."

"Why would you walk away from your dream to do this?"

Free's entire face filled with confusion, as if she spoke some alien language. "This was always my plan. I never considered an acting career."

"But I thought…you're always in costume and running to rehearsal. You never said…"

"I'm sorry, Sam. It didn't occur to me that you thought I planned to act for the rest of my life. I guess we never really talked about it."

"No, Free, we talked about plenty. You chose to leave that out. Why?"

"It wasn't intentional."

"You don't have to do a job just because your dad expects you to. You have a right to your own life and your own dreams."

He pressed his lips together and took her hand again. "Although my dad genuinely wants me to work for him, he never pressured me to do so. I like investing. From the time I was old enough to sit on my dad's lap and look at the *Wall Street Journal* with him, I knew I wanted a career in numbers."

She yanked her hand away. Betrayal washed over her. She had no idea who this man was, but he wasn't her boyfriend, Free. This was some slicked-up version of Humphrey. And she didn't think she liked him very much.

"What's wrong?"

"What's *wrong*?" Her voice rose and people turned to look at them. "My boyfriend turned out to be someone I don't even know."

Free grabbed her elbow. "Let's go to the hall and talk."

Before she could utter another word, he propelled her out to the lobby of the banquet hall. She yanked her arm back. "What is there to talk about?"

"Why are you so upset that you're causing a

scene at my dad's party?"

"You're just like them, but you had me convinced you were different. No wonder you were so worried about appearances and what your dad would think about my Reddit post."

Free raked a hand through his carefully styled hair. "I'm still the same guy I was yesterday."

"No, you're not. My Free would've been standing here dressed as Doctor Who with red gym shoes. My Free laughs and tells silly jokes and quotes movies, not stock market analyses."

He stepped closer, but she backed away. "I feel like everything was a lie."

"I never lied to you."

Her throat burned and tears pricked the backs of her eyes. "I need to leave."

"Let me drive you home."

"No. I'll call a cab." She held up a hand to keep him away. "Please just go back to your party."

He didn't move, so she did. She backed away to the coat check and bundled up quickly. She felt him staring at her, but he didn't attempt to stop her.

So she left.

FREE STOOD IN SHOCK AS SAM WALKED OUT OF THE building. He had no idea what had just happened. How did she not know he planned on being an investment banker? They'd talked about so much over the past few weeks, surely it had come up. He knew he told her about his classes. He remembered her wrinkling her nose at the thought of sitting through his Business Finance or Principles of Finance courses. What did she think he'd do with those classes?

He didn't know how long he stood staring after her, but he realized that his family would notice his absence. He walked back into the room and straight to the bar. A beer would no longer suit him. He ordered a Scotch and slammed it back. Then ordered another.

Cary came up next to him and slapped him on the back. "Might want to slow down. We still have hours to go."

"I won't make it for hours."

"Dad said your girlfriend is here. Where is she? I want to meet her."

"She left."

"Why?"

"I'm trying to figure that out. She was pissed off that I want to work for Dad and not be an actor." It sounded just as stupid out loud as it did in his head. He picked up his glass and drank.

Cary put his hand on Free's glass and forced it back down to the bar. "What?"

Free lifted a shoulder. "She thought Dad was forcing me to work for him. She said I should be able to follow my own dreams. When I told her this *was* my dream, she boiled."

"You've been dating this girl for weeks. You've spent the night with her and you never told her your career plans?"

"Apparently not." He tugged at the glass, but Cary wouldn't let it up.

"Dude, what the hell is wrong with you?"

"Me? I didn't do anything wrong. I showed up

to this damn party even though I didn't want to. I talked to people and did my level best not to embarrass myself. When my girlfriend appeared, I was relieved because I thought I'd have an ally in this mess. Besides you, that is. And instead, she yelled at me. Like really yelled. To the point that people started to stare." As soon as Cary's hand slipped from the lip of the glass, Free snatched it up and drained it.

"Getting drunk isn't going to solve this problem."

"I'm not getting drunk. I'm getting relaxed." He pushed the glass back toward the bartender. Cary was right. Getting drunk would only make things worse. However, the burn of alcohol in his system was a welcome feeling after the iciness he'd felt from Sam.

Cary ordered two glasses of water and then led Free away from the bar. "Let's get your mind off women for now. Focus on getting to know some clients. She'll need time to cool off and then you can call her and straighten things out."

As they wove through the throngs of guests, Free found it much easier to speak with people. He wasn't sure if it was the whiskey he'd consumed or if it was their consumption of alcohol, but conversation flowed freely. He'd carefully avoided the Wolfs so he wouldn't have to explain where Sam had gone or why.

Attempting to explain the situation to them would be even more awkward than telling Cary.

After an hour, he took a break and sent Sam a text to make sure she got home all right. He made the rounds to various groups of people and sat at a few tables to introduce himself. By the end of the night, he was once again feeling sober and thoughts of Sam crowded his head. She never answered his text.

The evening came to a close and the three Mitchell men waved good-bye to the last of the guests. They sat at a small round table and enjoyed a final glass of whiskey.

His dad raised his glass. "To a job well done. You made me proud tonight."

They toasted the successful party, but Free's mood was becoming foul.

"Pretty girl, your girlfriend," his dad commented.

"Yeah, she is."

"I didn't get a chance to see her again after we first met. Where'd she disappear to?"

"She left. We had a fight. Sort of." He looked at Cary. "You ready to go?"

"Yep."

They said good-bye to their parents and drove back to their apartment in silence. Before crawling into bed, Free called Sam, but she didn't answer. Since he didn't really know what to say, he didn't bother leaving a message.

CHAPTER ELEVEN

After fifteen phone calls, Free had given up. Sam wouldn't talk to him. He texted her the address to Hunter and Adam's place in case she still wanted to come to the party, but he wasn't counting on it. Although Hunter never agreed to a costume party, Free dressed as Doctor Who anyway. Usually, the clothes made him feel better, but not today.

He got to the apartment and helped Hunter and Adam clean up and move things around. Cary arrived with the keg and ice. Hunter focused on filling bowls with chips and dip. Cary said nothing, but patted Free's shoulder. Free never felt so depressed before and he'd been dumped plenty of times in his life.

People started to arrive for the party and Free tried to have fun, but all he could think about was Sam and why she wasn't coming.

Hunter came by with another bag of chips. "Where's your date?"

Free shrugged. "I don't know if she's coming.

She wouldn't return any of my calls for the last few days."

"What did you do?"

"I have no fucking clue. I ran into her at my dad's holiday party. She came with her parents. She seemed really upset to find out I planned to work at the investment firm after graduation. She was under the impression that my goal was to be an actor."

"Didn't you ever talk about your major? Careers? Anything? That's like basic level stuff."

"I don't know. She never asked, so I didn't offer. It's not like investment banking is an exciting topic for most people. If they don't ask, I don't mention it. Plus, our time together was always limited. Who wanted to talk about work?"

Hunter popped a tortilla chip in his mouth. "Let me guess. She saw the costumes and made the leap that acting is your passion."

"Not such a leap, but yeah. Looking back now, I can see where she made those assumptions and I didn't make the connection to correct her."

Hunter slapped a hand on his friend's shoulder. "Let me know if there's anything I can do to help. I hope she shows."

"Hope is a dangerous thing. Hope can drive a man insane."

"I know it's sad when you pull out *The Shawshank Redemption*."

Free did feel hopeless. Hard to imagine when just a few days ago he'd thought he met the perfect girl for him. He went to the kitchen to pour himself a beer.

A little more than an hour later and the party

was in full swing. Free had a few beers in him, but the alcohol didn't erase the depression he felt. He wanted to be a jolly drunk, but that didn't seem to be in the cards for him tonight.

He watched Adam draw on guests, mostly girls, giving them temporary tattoos, until he took off to hang out with his friend Reese. Free still questioned why she wasn't a real date for him.

"No sign of your girl yet?" Hunter asked.

"Nope."

"I have a favor to ask."

Free straightened. Anything to get his mind off Sam and his misery.

"Amy, Lisa, and Kelly are all here."

Free squinted in thought. "Ex-girlfriends?"

"Yeah and they won't leave. My new girlfriend, Sydney, will be here soon. I don't want them to cause trouble."

Free was taken aback by the troubled look in Hunter's eyes. Hunter normally liked the attention of as many females as he could find. "You really like this girl."

Free expected a joke, or for Hunter to at least scoff at him.

Instead, Hunter simply said, "Yeah." Then he pointed out the three girls.

Lisa was nearest to him, so Free grabbed his empty cup and strolled over. "Lisa?"

She turned and looked up at him with narrow eyes and a hint of a smirk. "Hi."

"Hi. I'm Free, a friend of Hunter's."

She looked him up and down. "What are you wearing?"

"I'm the Doctor."

She giggled. "Are you offering to play doctor with me?"

How could this girl already be buzzed? It was nowhere near midnight. "Maybe a little later. Can I get you a fresh drink? Maybe something to eat?"

She nodded and he held out his arm for her to walk to the kitchen. On the way, Free scanned the room to see whom he could foist Lisa off on. Near the keg, he saw Mike, one of the few marching band friends of Hunter's that he knew.

"Hey, Mike. Good to see you."

"Great party, as usual, man."

"Could you do me a favor? Lisa here needs a fresh drink."

Lisa looked up at him. "Mike will take care of you. I'll be back in a few minutes. I need to go check on something."

Mike gave him a thumbs-up and led Lisa to the keg.

Free ducked out of the kitchen and searched for either of the two other girls. Having a mission helped keep thoughts of Sam at bay. Unfortunately, Lisa hitting on him did nothing for him. He wasn't looking for a new date for the night. He simply had to keep a few girls away from his friend.

The living room had filled with people quickly as Hunter and his band started to play. Over the heads of the guests, Free saw a new addition to Hunter's band: a cute drummer. That must've been his girlfriend, the one he thought couldn't handle seeing the losing competition. She looked like she could hold her own as she beat away on her drums.

AS THE CAB DROVE THROUGH THE NEIGHBORHOOD toward the address Free had given her for the party, Sam tried to figure out exactly why she'd decided to go. He'd called and texted so many times over the last couple of days, but she didn't answer because she had no words. Jess had come over to keep her company and feed her an endless supply of ice cream.

Then she told Sam to get over it. As far as lies and betrayals go, Free's were pretty minor. They didn't feel minor to Sam, though. He was a corporate baboon in training. He planned to chase the dollar like so many other people.

The cab pulled up in front of a two-flat in a quiet family neighborhood. She could picture Free living in a place like this, but he'd said it was his friends' place.

She paid the cab driver and stared at the building.

"Are you getting out?"

Sam took a deep breath. "Yeah."

She climbed out and rushed up the stairs. Music and noise filtered through the door. She knocked and no one answered, so she tried the knob. It opened easily and she stepped in. She followed the noise into the first-floor apartment.

Warm air rushed over her. A band played in the living room. What should be the dining room held a couch and TV as well as a table filled with snacks. Sam stared at the crowd. When Free had invited her, she'd imagined a small gathering of his nerdy friends. She hadn't expected a raucous party.

She looked over the sea of people and caught a glimpse of Free. He was dressed as Doctor Who and her heart melted. She loved his dorkiness. Once again she was struck with questioning why she'd come. Had she planned to break up with him in person? She didn't have that kind of willpower when seeing him as the Doctor.

Edging along the wall, she tried to find a space to just think, but the noise was overwhelming.

"Samantha?"

Sam turned and looked at the man who'd called her. She didn't know him, but he looked vaguely familiar.

"It is you." He shook his head quickly. "I'm sorry. We've never actually met. I'm Cary. Free's brother."

Now she understood the familiarity. He had the same eyes and smile as Free. "Hi."

"Can I get you a drink?"

"No. Uh…I was just trying to find a place to think for a minute. I don't even know if I belong here." She felt like she was yelling even as he lowered his body to hear her.

He crooked his finger at her and led her back out the front door. Although the thumping beat could be felt out here, the door kept the majority of noise at bay.

"I'm glad you came tonight. Free has been really bummed since the office party."

"So I guess he told you everything."

"Kind of. He's confused and not sure why you got so mad."

Sam bit her lip. "I'm not entirely sure myself. I feel like he lied to me about who he is."

Cary sat on the steps leading to the upstairs apartment and patted the step next to him. She sat.

"Tell me what happened."

"Nothing happened. I met this great guy who made me laugh and dressed in silly costumes to make his brother's life easier. He turned out to be something different."

"He's the same guy."

Sam shook her head. She wanted to believe that she'd been falling for the real Free, but she couldn't get the image of him as a banker out of her mind.

"You have to understand that the office party was hard for Free. He doesn't like the bullshit end of dealing with clients. He wants to run the numbers and make them money. Me, on the other hand, I like the wining and dining aspect. He put on the face he needed to for the party."

So he'd been playing a character like any other role. "But he said his dream is to be a banker like your dad."

"He does want to do that. Is there something wrong with wanting to make money and build a good life?"

"No. It sounds crazy when you put it like that."

"It sounds crazy because it is crazy. I'll tell you the truth. I've never seen Free so into a girl before. He's been moping around not knowing what to do."

"I haven't been much better. I've been trying to sort this out in my head."

"What did you come up with?"

Sam shrugged.

"Why did you come here tonight?"

"I don't know. The whole way here, I tried to figure it out. I needed to come. Part of me thought I would look at him and want to break up with him. But then I saw him. He's Doctor Who. That's the guy I fell for." She slumped over and held her head.

"If you care about him—and it's pretty obvious you do—why do you care what he does for a living, especially if he likes it?"

"I don't want to be married to a guy like my dad."

Cary laughed. "Don't they say that girls grow up to do just that? I know your dad through work. He seems like a good guy. Dedicated, hardworking. He sucks at golf, so he's not infallible. And he loves his daughter."

Sam's head snapped up and she stared at Cary.

"He's talked about you at every meeting we've ever had." He opened his arms. "I guess he is like Free because that guy hasn't been able to shut up about you."

"Really?"

Cary nodded. "You know, *it doesn't matter if the guy is perfect or if the girl is perfect, as long as they are perfect for each other.*"

"Do you steal movie quotes, too?"

"*Good Will Hunting.* I thought Free would appreciate it."

Sam stood.

"You decided something?"

She smiled and nodded. "*I'm going to make him an offer he can't refuse.*"

Cary barked out a laugh that echoed through the hall. "I don't know if it's in Free's best interest that you just quoted *The Godfather.*"

Sam smiled. "Thanks."

"Anytime."

She turned and went back into the party to find Free.

FREE ROAMED THROUGH THE APARTMENT, UNABLE to find Kelly. He hoped Adam had had better luck in distracting Hunter's former girlfriends. As he squeezed behind a couple making out, he caught sight of something familiar, a waterfall of brown hair that had him spinning to make sure he hadn't imagined it. Could it be that Sam had come?

But when he turned, he saw nothing. He crossed the room to where he thought he saw her. Nothing. He rubbed his eyes. How sad was it that he'd been reduced to imagining his girlfriend?

Cary came up next to him and bumped his shoulder. "Did Samantha find you?"

"What? She's here?"

Cary nodded.

Free left him standing there and pushed through the bodies and had zero luck finding her. Finally, he gave up and fought his way back to the living room, where Hunter's band played. He strode up to Hunter and tapped his shoulder. When Hunter leaned over, Free yelled, "I need the mike."

Hunter nodded and waved Lance over, who brought the microphone with him.

Free took a deep breath and brought the microphone to his mouth. "Excuse me. Sam? Samantha Wolf. If you're still here, please come to the front. Sam?"

On the other end of the room, near the kitchen, he saw an arm in the air. Then the crowd parted, creating a path between him and Sam. He handed Lance the mike and stepped forward.

The band picked up where they'd left off, but the crowd watched his progress toward Sam before swallowing the empty space behind him. When he reached her, he asked, "What are you doing here?

"I needed to see you."

Oh crap. She came to break up with him in person. He was going to need a whole lot more alcohol if this was how he was going to spend midnight. He reached for her hand and tugged her toward Adam's bedroom. He closed the door behind them. "Before you say anything, please hear me out."

She opened her mouth, but he held up a hand to silence her.

"I never meant to lie to you. We talked about the classes I was taking and I kind of thought they were self-explanatory. You made some assumptions about me and I didn't correct you. That doesn't make me a liar. I would never lie to you." He shoved his hands in his pockets and gripped his Doctor Who screwdriver, hoping it would bring him luck.

"I know. I felt betrayed when I saw you at the party. All of a sudden you weren't my quirky boyfriend anymore. You were like my dad." She started to pace and twisted her hands together. "I love my dad. But even from an early age, I knew that money was really important to him. Not more important than his family, but a very close second. It's like he couldn't be truly happy without money. And he uses that money to"—she continued with air quotes—"take care of me."

She stepped closer. "I don't want to be with a guy who overvalues money. I knew that wasn't the case with you as an actor. Most actors don't make it big. They do it because of love. I want to be with someone who loves what he does."

"I do. I love figuring out how to make money for other people. I make money in the process. I also love acting, but that's my break from the real world. I never wanted it to be my real world. I need the security of a regular paycheck, something I can count on. Acting can't do that for me. I would end up resenting it."

He adjusted his tie and searched for a way to explain. He filled his lungs and spoke again. "Acting is my release. I can be comfortable in whatever character I choose to be. But I need to keep the two parts of my life separate. I guess that in doing that, I neglected to fill you in on a huge part of me."

She nodded and went back to pacing. She paused near the pile of coats on Adam's bed. "It's important to me that you tell me things. That you don't leave them out because you think it's boring or I won't care. I want to know all of you. I'm not sure if I can get used to the banker you. I like the actor you."

He moved closer and reached out, smoothing

his hand down her hair. "Does that mean we still have a chance?"

She nodded and pulled him in by his tie. She pressed a quick kiss to his lips. "I want to be your Rose, Doctor. Your companion wherever you travel."

Free slid a hand over her hip. "Did you watch more of my favorite show?"

She grinned as she wrapped her arms around his neck. "I had to see what all the fuss was about."

"And?"

"And I decided that the Doctor needed Rose as much as she needed him, even though they were so very different."

"It is gonna be fantastic!"

"Kiss me, you fool."

"Hey, using quotes are my thing."

"Not anymore."

She pulled him closer until their mouths connected and no more words were needed. Having Samantha as his companion was more than he could've dreamed of.

AUTHOR'S NOTE

If you liked *His Dream Role*, don't miss *His Work of Art* and *His New Jam*, available now! Turn the page for an excerpt from *His Work of Art* and *His New Jam* in case you missed them. If you've enjoyed reading about my nerds, I would appreciate it if you could leave a brief review.

Also, sign up for my newsletter to get a free epilogue to catch up with our nerds after graduation.

Be sure to also check out the first Hot & Nerdy trilogy as well as Shannyn Schroeder's contemporary romance series, The O'Learys:

More Than This
A Good Time
Something to Prove
Catch Your Breath
Just a Taste
Hold Me Close

HIS WORK OF ART

*A*dam Hayes stared at the black line drawing and wished for more inspiration. Something was off, but he couldn't quite figure it out. He'd thought that going over the pencil with ink would spark something, but he was still at a loss.

He normally enjoyed days like this at the comics shop. The periodic customer would break the monotony of his frozen brain, but the store was quiet enough that he could get some drawing done.

The masked superhero stared at him. Maybe if it was in color. In Adam's mind, he saw dark skin and darker eyes.

But skin tone and eye color wouldn't give him a name.

The door chimed and Adam looked up to see his friend, Free, walking in. Even from the other side of the store, Adam felt the temperature drop with the blast of cold air that followed Free.

"Hey, man, what's up?" Free called out.

"Nothing." Adam gathered his pages and

stacked them on the edge of the table. He walked to the counter to meet Free and took in his appearance. Brown tweed hat and long overcoat. "Meeting Cary at the gym?"

"No, I'm walking around looking like Sherlock Holmes because I thought it would be a good way to pick up a girl."

"It might work. You have a bit of Benedict Cumberbatch going on."

Free threw one of the gloves he'd just removed at Adam. It flopped on the counter.

"Last time I saw Cary he looked good. I thought you were done dressing up to get him through the workouts."

"I probably could be. I think it's mostly habit now. He's come a long way, and I don't want him to lose motivation. Plus, I have an excuse to dress up."

"You say shit like that and then you wonder why chicks think you're gay."

Free rolled his eyes. Adam liked to give him a hard time. For most of his life, Free was a strait-laced banker-in-training, but his love of the theater had allowed him to become anyone he wanted.

Adam envied that skill.

"Where's Hunter? I thought you said three thirty."

"He's late, like always."

The door swung open again and Hunter strode in.

"Why did I have to come here if we're just talking about the New Year's Eve party? Couldn't we do this at home later?"

"Free has to meet Cary at the gym."

"Then I have rehearsal," Free added.

"Why couldn't it wait? We have like a month before the party." He tucked his hands into the beat-up black leather jacket that he'd been wearing since high school.

Free straightened. "We need to talk about invitations. We don't want a repeat of last year."

"Why not? Last year was epic."

Adam crossed his arms. "Your word-of-mouth campaign led to an apartment full of strangers."

"They weren't all strangers."

"Just the entire marching band."

"Not all of the band came, and it was fun."

"Except for all the drunk bodies laying all over the place the following morning."

Free held up his hands. "I can't say much about that since I don't live with you guys and therefore don't suffer those repercussions, but I agree that it was too crowded to actually have fun with friends."

Adam pointed at Hunter. "And don't forget the catfight that broke out."

"That wasn't my fault. I'm irresistible." Hunter's gaze bounced back and forth between them. "Does that mean you guys are going to have dates this year?"

"Nope," Adam answered. Somehow, he'd always managed to not have a girlfriend over the holidays. It wasn't like he planned it.

Free looked anywhere but at Hunter.

Hunter sighed. "You guys are pitiful. The epitome of nerds. You get dates, I won't tell everyone and their cousin to come to our party."

"You have a date?" Free asked.

Hunter smiled. "Not yet. I have plenty of time. Working on some options."

Hunter was always investigating his options. The door chimed, and Reese walked through the door with a smile on her face.

"Hi, Reese."

She pulled up short and her eyes widened as she took Adam in, standing with his friends. She took a sharp left and started thumbing through a bin of comics.

Hunter looked at him with eyes almost as wide as Reese's. He then waved a hand toward Reese.

"What?" Adam whispered.

"Ask her, you idiot. She's cute."

"She's not like that."

Hunter shook his head. "Every girl is dateable."

Free checked his watch. "As much as I love your verbal advice column, I have to head out to meet Cary. If I'm not there before him, he might chicken out." He tugged his gloves back on and went to the door. Over his shoulder, he called, "See you later."

Hunter zipped up his jacket. To Adam, he said, "See you at home?"

"Yeah. After closing." He occasionally took the closing shift so his mom could have a free night, and it worked well with his class schedule.

Another customer walked in as Hunter left. Adam was almost able to forget Reese's presence, except now Hunter had put the idea of asking her out in his head. He shoved the thought aside and greeted his customer. "Anything special you're looking for today?"

"My son is eight and I want to get him some comics. But you know, I don't want to spend an arm and a leg because he's eight. He hasn't quite grasped the idea of taking care of his books."

"There are lots of books for kids. We have a clearance section over here." He led the way to the small bin and helped the guy pick out a few comics. Then he went back to his station behind the register to ring him up.

"Wow! You're actually good."

Adam glanced over his shoulder at hearing Reese—words of surprise no guy ever wanted to hear—to see that she stood over his drawing table. Invading his space behind the counter. He thanked the customer in front of him and handed him his bag of comic books. He watched the customer leave before walking up behind Reese.

"Could you—" He gestured to the other side of the counter, the storefront for customers.

She shrugged. "Oh, sorry." She moved to the other side, but continued talking. "It's just that I see you drawing all the time. I wanted to check it out."

Adam moved his panels and sheets of paper back to the order in which he had them. Even if he were to invite her to look at his work, he wouldn't let her shuffle them like a deck of cards. Although she was now standing six feet away, he could still smell her lingering scent. Something soft, but he couldn't quite place it. He found it distracting.

While he continued to straighten his table, he asked, "Is there something you needed help finding?"

It was a ridiculous question because she was

able to find things in the small store as easily as he could. She'd been coming in at least once a week for months, ever since one of their competitors had shut down. Reese had strolled in looking for the latest *Batgirl* comic and his life hadn't been the same since.

"So what are you drawing?"

"Nothing special. Just working up some ideas."

"Those aren't random doodles. I know a superhero when I see one. Who is he?"

Adam set his papers back on the desk. He rubbed the back of his neck, irritation grinding into his muscles. "He doesn't have a name. Not yet anyway."

"He's pretty awesome. You need to name him."

"Yeah, I'll get right on that." As if he hadn't already spent his entire afternoon doing just that. He crossed his arms. "So what are you here for today? You picked up all of your regular issues earlier this week."

"I came to see you." She leaned forward on the counter in front of the register. "I have a proposition for you."

At least these were better words to hear than her first statement. He joined her and braced his palms on the glass and waited.

"I have to do a senior project. My plan is to publish an anthology of comics."

They'd talked about comics plenty over the months. They both had strong opinions, and he enjoyed arguing with her. He also knew that she was a writer, not that he'd ever read any of her stuff.

"And?" he prompted.

"I need an artist. I have most of the stories done." She tilted her head side to side, her straight dark hair swaying with the movement. Squinting her eyes, she said, "Well, they need polishing and maybe some revising, but I figure they'll get fine-tuned as we get to the storyboard phase."

"We?" No way was she asking what he thought.

"If you agree to be my partner, yeah, *we*. I'm under a bit of a time crunch because I have to have things in place to start my crowd-funding campaign. So it'll be a lot of work, but you'll get paid. At least you will if the campaign gets funded. Plus, I figure we have holiday break coming up so we won't have to worry about classes."

"You want me to illustrate your comics?" The thought was a massive blur in his brain. Working together on a comic was intense. He doubted they could get along long enough to complete anything. They managed to argue about just about everything related to comics.

"Yeah. I had the idea a couple of weeks ago when I saw you working at your table. You were so passionate and into it, that it swallowed you. I get like that when I'm in the zone writing. I need that kind of partner." Her stormy blue eyes focused intently on him from beneath her shaggy bangs.

"Do I really need to point out that we don't get along?"

In truth, Reese was one of his all-time favorite customers. She was smart and argued with passion. It was almost enough for him to forgive her for choosing DC over Marvel.

"Who said we have to get along? I'm an excellent writer. From what I can see there, you're an excellent artist. Together, we can put together a fabulous book. " She leaned closer, almost to his side of the counter. "Afraid you can't handle me?"

He chuckled. "Sorry to disappoint, but you don't scare me. However, I don't like to waste my time."

She eased back. "How about this? You can read the story for the first book. Then make your decision. But it'll have to be fast because I have to have everything in place before my campaign goes live. The book doesn't need to be complete, but I have to have enough to entice people to back me."

The idea intrigued him, but Reese would never have been his first choice for a partner. Getting paid to draw was exactly what he was looking for. And if her campaign got fully funded, he would have a publication credit to his name. Having experience like that would help as he started his job hunt after graduation. "Bring it by. I'll take a look."

Her face lit up almost as brightly as when she'd tried to convince him that Batman was better than Iron Man. "Excellent." She reached into her messenger bag and pulled out a purple folder. "Here you go."

He eyed the folder. "You were that sure that I'd say yes?"

She winked at him. "I was cautiously optimistic."

He reached for the folder, but she tugged it back.

"For your eyes only."

The guarded look in her eye made him pause. Who the hell did she think he would show this to?

"Got it." He accepted the folder. "When do you need an answer?"

"The sooner the better. I need to get moving."

"Okay. I'll have a decision by next week when you come in for your books."

She pulled a pen from one of the many pockets of her cargo pants, snatched the folder back, and scribbled on the cover. "Here's my number. Call me if you decide before then and we can come up with a plan."

He stared at the number on the folder. "Okay."

"See ya later, Cap'n."

He shot her a dirty look. He hated the nickname she'd given him, Captain. When she first called him Captain, he'd assumed it was after Captain America, but she'd informed him that she went with a DC hero, Captain Atom, whose human last name was Adam. He liked her playfulness, but she could've chosen a cooler hero.

HIS NEW JAM

Sydney shoved another spoonful of cereal into her mouth and stared at the calendar. Two weeks. That's all she had left to suffer through until marching band was over for the year. Two weeks of practice and drills and football games. Then she could pack up the fucking cymbals until next summer.

Her older sister, Trisha, came into the kitchen still in her robe. "Aren't you going to be late?"

"Whatever." Sydney slurped at her milk to prevent Trish from nagging again. They were both well aware she needed the scholarship the marching band gave her for school. It didn't mean Syd had to like it.

"I don't see what's so bad about band. You get to play the instrument you love. The music's not all bad. So the uniforms are a little dorky, but you look good on the field." Trisha poured herself a cup of coffee.

"I don't get to play the instrument I love. I play the damn cymbals. Just once I would like to be given an actual drum. I sucked it up last year as the new kid, waiting, thinking that at some point, as guys graduate, I could step up. Instead, it's this patronizing attitude. The drums are heavy. They'll be awkward. There are already other players waiting. But the worst is that I'm so good at the cymbals, they don't want to lose me." She dumped her bowl in the sink. "It's all bullshit. I don't even know why I need to finish school. I want to play. I don't need a degree to do that."

Trisha sighed the same way their mom always had. "We made a deal with Dad. You get to live with me in the city as long as you're in school."

"That was when I was underage. I'm twenty-one. I can live wherever I want."

Trish patted her arm. "But you don't want to let Dad down. Suck it up. Only another year and a half until graduation. Only a few weeks until you can forget about band for a while."

It annoyed her how well her sister knew her. Of course she wouldn't let their dad down. He'd decided the only way for them to have a good life was to go to college, as if college could solve every problem. He held fast to the idea that if he had gone to college, his life, and by extension their lives, would've been so much easier.

So she was in school, getting a graphic design degree that would be useless because all she wanted to do was play music. Real music, rock, with a band, for an audience that wanted to hear it.

But Trish did have a point: Only a few weeks and she could say good-bye to being out in the cold, stomping on hard grass, pretending to enjoy herself during a football game. She tossed her backpack into her car and drove to the field. She shoved a hat on her head and grabbed her cymbals from the trunk. Just as she slammed the lid down, someone whistled at her.

Sydney's head popped up, ready to berate whatever asshole thought it was okay to catcall, when she saw her friend Emma running down the aisle of cars. She skidded to a halt in front of Sydney. "Whoa. You look ready to bite someone's head off."

"I thought you were some guy whistling at me."

"Lighten up. So what if I was? You look ready to commit bodily harm."

"I'm just extra cranky. It's cold and I want the season to be over. Plus, it's a new week, so that tenor hasn't done his shit yet."

"What?"

"You know who I'm talking about. The tenor sax guy who hits on anything female. Every week since the summer, I can't walk by without him playing some song at me."

Emma smirked. "How do you know he's playing for you?"

They headed toward the field together. "He stands off to the side and waits for me to get within ten feet before playing a note. Trust me, he's flirting, in his own lame way."

Emma nudged her shoulder. "His name is Hunter. He's a huge flirt, but totally harmless. He's having fun. He does it to make people smile. No one takes him seriously. As far as I know, he's never dated anyone from band. Plus, he's cute."

Emma had her there. The guy was cute, but even Syd knew he had a reputation for dating around a lot. She hadn't given him too much thought. Okay, that was a lie. Last season she crushed on him pretty hard, but he hadn't given her a second glance. She had no idea what had changed, but these past few months had been torturous.

She had no desire to waste her time on a fling with some guy who would toss her aside next week. "Does anyone ever flirt back? Maybe that's why he doesn't date anyone."

"Oh, no, plenty flirt back. It's a game to keep things fun. How could you not have caught on?"

"It wasn't included in band camp." Sydney wasn't quite sure what to do with that. They neared the mob of people that would turn into organized rows of musicians. Sure enough, Tenor Guy stood off to the side, staring in her direction even as he carried on a conversation with another sax player.

He said nothing as he brought his instrument up and played the first notes. Syd continued walking, trying to ignore him. She got a few feet past him when the notes of his song bounced through her mind and recognition hit. He was playing the damn Disney song, "Let It Go."

Oh, yeah, this guy was hilarious. So he thought she was an ice queen. He got close to the chorus and Syd paused mid-stride. Just as the ice queen accepted her fate, Sydney clashed her cymbals together and winked over her shoulder at Hunter. She was fine with being cold.

<u>**Daring Divorcees Series**</u>

One Night with a Millionaire

My Best Friend's Ex

My Forever Plus-One